The Pirate Queen

A Thrilling Teenage Adventure

by Colin Vard

Celtpress Ltd.

Celtpress Ltd.
Kindlestown Hill
Delgany
Co. Wicklow
Republic of Ireland
Tel/Fax: (01) 287 3026

ISBN 1-897973-03-9

© 1994 Celtpress Ltd.
All rights reserved. No part of this publication may be
reproduced, stored in a retrieval system, or transmitted in
any form or by any means electronic, mechanical,
photocopying, recording, or otherwise, without prior
written permission of the publisher.

Printed by Vision Print
Unit 3, Blackrock Business Centre
Brookfield Terrace
Blackrock, Co. Dublin

I would like to take this opportunity to thank all the bookshops and their knowledgeable and hard-working staff for their invaluable support and co-operation in stocking and promoting Celtales children's books. Without your help these books would never have been published!
Thank you sincerely.

*I dedicate this book to **Rita Hughes**, an outstanding woman who embodies the same spirit, energy and determination as that notorious sea captain Grace O'Malley.*

Illustrations by Tony Kew

CHAPTER 1

One afternoon in Mountclare School infirmary, Grainne discovered an ancient key hidden in a statue. This key unlocked a door to the past. Grainne opened the door and travelled back in time to Dublin in 1916.

*In **Blood Beyond the Keyhole**, Grainne lived with the Countess Markievicz and witnessed the horrors and futility of a people's rising littered with misfortune, insanity and crime.*

Mountclare Castle, January 1593

I stood rigid, washed by a cold animal fear. Somewhere in the chilly bowels of the castle a large door creaked on rusted hinges. A hostile gust of wind cut through the damp corridor and mercilessly gnawed at my bones. Somehow, by passing back through the door, I had travelled further back in time.

In a room above, a group of men conversed happily in a strange tongue. Transfixed and bewildered, I observed through the half opened door three characters flirting theatrically around a blazing fire. Two men hovered, their faces painted, powdered and blushed by the roaring log fire. They were as womanly in appearance and manner as the young distinguished lady they endeavoured to entertain.

The eldest and most hideous looking was dressed in a red silk jacket with black pantaloons trimmed in gold brocade. He squinted lecherously as he removed a monocle from his jacket and positioned it deep in the socket of his right eye. He proceeded to examine in detail one of the many sparkling jewels which emblazoned the young woman's ample bosom.

The younger man, indifferent and more elegantly dressed, wore a yellow padded waistcoat over a white doublet sleeved shirt with matching yellow fringed pantaloons. His jacket of black velvet was trimmed with gold ties. Displaying a disturbing effeminate mannerism, he slowly and deliberately folded back a long lace cuff from his wrist and played with a perfumed handkerchief. Both men wore outrageous blonde wigs powdered in an exotic blue tint.

The scent of musk and apple blossom from the dry, sparking logs drifted through the open door. The young woman, beautified by gold and sparkling diamonds, ran a slender, manicured hand through flowing nut-brown hair flecked in semi-precious stones and beads. Her personality shone like a star; she was courteous and dignified.

Tiring of the older man's ill-favoured advances, she turned, shrugged her shoulders in a very definite gesture of annoyance and glided across the room, her delicate, pale, silk dress shimmering in the soft candle light. Undeterred by this rebuke, the man mindlessly trailed the woman across the flagstone floor. Angered by his continuing insensitivity, the young woman struck out at her tormentor and ran towards the door. Coming swiftly to my senses, I turned and searched for a place to hide.

"Máire, tar anseo gan mhoill!" the woman called out.

Behind me was a rough-cut stone staircase. It was lit by a winding, flickering row of candles leading, I presumed, up to the castle battlements and down to a cold dank dungeon. A door above opened and a woman's gentle footsteps approached.

"Tá mé ag teacht," a girl's voice echoed through the castle.

This strange tongue, I quickly deduced, was Gaelic!

"Máire, tar anseo gan mhoill!"

"Mary, come here immediately!"

I ran blindly and without due caution down the stone steps. Behind me, a heavy latch was drawn back and a door began to creak open. As I turned to look, I missed my footing on the uneven steps and fell headlong down into the eerie darkness. Above me a man's voice shouted in Gaelic.

"Cé atá ann?"

I lay in silence, trembling in pain and fear. Warm blood trickled from my temple and stung my eyes. I dared not move. The voice called out again.

"Cé atá ann?"

My head rested awkwardly on a cold stone step. To my horror, a black rat appeared at my shoulder. I froze while his damp, foul-smelling fur brushed against my ear. As if in defiance, he scuttled over my hand, his bony tail running between my fingers. Annoyed by the animal's insolence, I struck the offender firmly on its hindquarters, sending it crashing against the castle wall. It squealed loudly in shock and pain then shuffled off indignantly into the darkness.

"Damn vermin," said the man above.

Assured that it was safe to proceed, I removed the sweat and grime from my brow. Fortunately, nothing was broken, least of all my resolve. Leaning against the damp outer wall of the castle, I worked my way timidly down to the ground floor. To my horror, the door leading from the castle to the ramparts was almost two feet thick, securely bolted, padlocked and guarded by sleeping dogs! I panicked and moved defensively back up the stairs. The dogs sensed my intrusion and fear. They began to whimper and pull against their chains. Agitated, they began to bark.

I ran blindly back up the stone steps. My heart was pumping violently. On a dark landing, in the fading glimmer of candlelight, I viewed a small opening in the outer wall. A gentle sea breeze brushed against my cheek. In the distance, I could hear the welcome sound of breakers crashing on the strand.

I reached out into the cold night. A long timber beam extended beyond the castle wall. A rope was attached to a primitive pulley. I had no alternative; I leaned out and grasped the rope.

Behind, in the basement, I could hear the dogs baying and pulling furiously at their chains. I secured the rope around my waist. A door creaked opened below. Men were shouting instructions in Gaelic. The hounds were released from their shackles and bounded up the stairs. Taking a deep breath, I eased myself out into the empty darkness. I tugged hopefully on the rope.

The grotesque, snarling jaw of an enormous Irish wolfhound grasped the hem of my dress and began to drag me back through the opening. Behind, assorted growling hounds were trying to clamber over their cohorts to reach their prey.

I had no choice. I leaned backwards into the void. Gathering all my mental and physical strength, I kicked out at the wolfhound and launched myself into the darkness. As I tumbled backwards, the rope, to my horror, fell freely with me. The cold air whistled by my ears. I braced myself, fearing I would surely be smashed to pieces on the rocks surrounding the base of the castle.

The next thing I remember was struggling in confusion to catch my breath in the stagnant waters of the castle moat.

I gathered my senses and swam to the bank. Above, the dogs continued to howl. I stood frigid on the rampart, now wise to the fact that a moat was not only a means of defence; it was also a method of disposing of human excrement. … My skin crawled!

Above, at the opening in the castle wall, a man's face appeared. I stood motionless. I was cold, wet and confused. After scouring the ramparts for a few moments, the man's eyebrows narrowed and he pointed triumphantly in my direction.

I turned, ran around the castle ramparts and hurried across the open fields. With a rising sea breeze at my back and the moon as a guide, I made rapid progress across the wet, muddy fields. Great herds of cattle and sheep scattered in all directions. I ran towards the shadows of the distant mountains and woods. Behind, on the ramparts, men and dogs shouted and barked excitedly. The hunt was about to begin and I was to be their prey.

The dogs were unleashed and within moments were closing on me. They were no more than a hundred yards behind. I could hear the mongrel pack of hounds growling, snorting and barking in unison. In the corner of my eye something moved. I stopped. An animal pricked up its ears. It was a horse. It tensed noticeably as I approached. To my dismay, it pivoted on its hind legs and galloped off towards the oak trees.

The strange mixture of hounds now circled me menacingly. I was terrified. Their handlers were too far behind to exert any calming influence on these wild, snarling animals. Some of the braver dogs moved forward, growling and snapping at my heels. They were primed; one move and I was dead. Like coiled springs they swayed back and forward on their hind legs, staring at me with their mad eyes.

5

Across on the other side of the field, the horse galloped on towards the forest. As he approached the undergrowth, a startled stag raised his head and snorted in fear. The dogs immediately picked up the scent of the frightened animal and, to my relief, took chase.

Reprieved, and with a singular objective, I hurried on through sodden fields and rivers, observed by curious foxes, badgers and owls. My progress was aided by a clear sky and a glorious moon that lead me towards the dark, forbidding mountains and stars.

Hours later, exhausted, I sat on a rock close to a riverbank. I examined the wounds I had accumulated running through thickets of scrub and gorse. My hands, face and legs were veiled in blood. My muscles and lungs ached. I removed my boots. My hair and clothes were damp and soaked in slime, sweat and foul-smelling excrement. I was in total mental and physical disarray.

As the sun began to rise, I eased back on the rock and, resting my head on a damp clump of moss, … slept.

CHAPTER 2

To my astonishment, I awoke lying on a sack of fresh-smelling ferns nestling among the bog oak rafters of a small labourer's cottage. Hushed voices below spoke in Gaelic.

Curious to explore my new environment, I raised my head. Through the haze of smoke rising from the smouldering turf fire, I could distinguish a thick-set man in concerned conversation with a gaunt young woman breast-feeding a baby.

I lay awhile absorbing my new surroundings and the pending necessity to converse in Gaelic.

The man was employed as a farm labourer by the Chieftain Fiach MacHugh, leader of the O'Byrne clan. He was in distress after failing to provide sufficient crops for the chieftain in lieu of rent for the last quarter.

Outside, it began to rain heavily. I pulled a heavy wool blanket round my shoulders. I observed the rainwater as it soaked through the straw thatch and ran slowly along the dried potato stalks securing the thatch to the rafters.

The man complained bitterly, suggesting that MacHugh should be governed by a higher, more amenable authority. As artisans, he said, they had no recourse to seek justice.

"We are itinerant labourers," he continued, "free to

seek seasonal and permanent employment. If we stay longer upon this desolate mountain, we will surely starve. I cannot allow my child and wife to endure further hardship. Prepare yourself, woman. At first light we move south to Wexford."

"This is an inopportune time to move," the woman argued strongly and dismissively. "The winter months are upon us now. The child is not yet three months and still suckling. She will perish on such a hazardous journey. Should we survive the elements, we will surely be easy prey for hungry thieves, wolves and vagabonds. Be mindful, too, that MacHugh, if he takes it upon himself, will dispatch soldiers to exact retribution. He is a vindictive, evil man who shows no mercy to man or beast."

"I have spoken, woman!"

The room became silent. I turned on my side and idly poked a hole in the outer wall, which was constructed from a mixture of mud kneaded with straw. As I lay, tearful and confused, a hand came from behind and tenderly stroked my hair. I jumped in fright and turned to face my comforter.

He was tall, broad-shouldered and no more than thirty years old. This harsh life had made an old man of him. His hands were deformed and callused. His face was stained and cracked with smoke and honest toils endured in the severest of weathers. He smiled a toothless grin through a matted ginger beard. He gestured for me to follow him down the ladder. I sat up, removed the heavy wool rug and followed.

Despite the smouldering turf fire, the cottage was cold and damp. The smoke stung my eyes while the wet and uneven clay floor stuck uncomfortably to my bare feet. My old clothes had been discarded and I was dressed in a simple black gown with a crimson petticoat. The woman

8

handed me a shawl and smiled as she pointed to my feet.

"You have come from a privileged background, Miss. Your tender feet, it is plain to see, have not been exposed to hardship. My name is Bridget, the child is Eimear and this is my husband, Brendan. You were found yesterday at midday, down by the banks of the Avonbeg river. You were in a sorry state and fortunate to be alive.

"You must rest now. Tomorrow, we will decide what is best for you. What do they call you?"

"Grainne," I answered feebly.

Back in the security of the rafters, with a honey-flavoured milk drink, I considered the tiny cottage. The reason for the abundance of oppressive smoke was the absence of a chimney. The burning logs were situated in a iron grate in the centre of the room. Suspended over the smoking fire was a black iron pot of simmering water. In all the time I spent in the cottage, the fire was never extinguished. It was the provider of light, heat and sustenance.

I heard voices outside. The door of the cottage suddenly opened. The wind and rain howled angrily and blew through the opening as Brendan went outside. The loose thatch above my head fluttered. … I slept.

At dawn the next morning, I was awoken by Eimear crying. A candle was lit. Brendan dressed while Bridget fed the baby. I climbed down from the rafters. The floor was wet. Outside, the rain had stopped. The sun was rising and the room began to brighten. Without speaking, Brendan put on a sleeveless, homespun wool cloak, bowed his head and disappeared out the front door. On his shoulder was an axe.

There was little furniture in the cottage except for two stools, a bench and a crude wooden cradle. Bridget tidied away the rough animal skins on which she and Brendan slept. She was dressed in rags. Her feet were swollen and deformed. The clothes she had graciously given me were obviously her best. They were clean, but made from a very harsh wool that had been homespun and dyed.

Brendan returned shortly with wood for the fire and milk for the table. He stoked the embers and left the cottage again. ... He looked worried.

Bridget placed coarse brown bread, cheese, buttermilk and honey on the table. She broke the bread and placed it on a wooden platter along with a piece of cheese. Then she took a wooden bowl and poured in some buttermilk and honey. She then placed the plate and bowl before me. While I ate, she spoke.

"Grainne, Brendan and I have spoken at length. We consider that we have done our duty. Like an injured bird with a broken wing, we took you in. Now that you are strong enough, you must be returned to the wild. We are but a poor labouring family, scratching an existence on the five acre plot MacHugh has granted us. On this land, we must grow and provide vegetables for the chieftain's table. Over the past months, the ground has been ravished by storms and rain. Underground springs have erupted and flowed through the land. The crops for MacHugh's table now lie rotten in the ground, as does our bleak future."

The door swung open. Brendan stood, destitute, in the open doorway.

"The crops have been destroyed," he exclaimed. "The Avonbeg ... It has burst its banks! Bridget, what am I to do? I cannot stem the tide of nature with my bare hands! ... We are lost! ... I have failed my young wife and child. MacHugh will exact his revenge. Nothing is surer!"

Brendan walked to the fire and fell to his knees. He stared silently at the flames.

As his head sank to his chest, the door burst open. Standing in the doorway was a tall, broad-shouldered man with a ruddy complexion. His long, matted straw-coloured hair fell to his shoulders and was styled with a jagged fringe. His trousers were brown, his shirt white with mutton leg sleeves. His shoes were of fine leather. In his belt, he had a knife with a curved blade. His woollen cloak had a fur collar and trailed along the ground. Behind him stood a group of uniformed foot soldiers. Some carried long swords and crossbows, others spears. All wore heavy, pleated wool tunics falling just below their knees. On their feet they wore leather sandals covered in sheep skin. Their helmets had a single horn in the centre.

"Brendan McMahon, you are charged with failing to pay rent to your landlord, the Chieftain Fiach MacHugh. I am ordered to take you from this place and deliver you this day to the mercy of your master in Ballinacor House."

The man stood back. On his command, two soldiers entered the cottage and raised Brendan roughly from his kneeling position and marched him outside. Four soldiers solemnly escorted Brendan away from the cottage.

Bridget and I followed. The cold, harsh daylight hurt my eyes. It was freezing. I had never known cold like it. The landscape was white and brittle. Bridget was distraught. She wrapped Eimear securely in a fringed woollen blanket, then placed the baby on her back. She implored the captain for mercy. He turned away and issued further orders.

"Burn the cabin!"

The three remaining soldiers moved into the cottage. Moments later, Bridget and Brendan's furniture, possessions and home were engulfed in flames.

I was frozen. My whole body shook uncontrollably. My feet were bare, numb and beginning to swell. I, too, was homeless. For the moment, to survive, I had to befriend these wretched people. I ran to catch up with the procession to Ballinacor House.

CHAPTER 3

The walk to Ballinacor House was a woeful, distressing experience. As we walked from the smouldering remains of the cottage, it began to rain - a damp mist, at first, that gave way to a relentless downpour. The mountain submitted and was enveloped in a thick grey cloud.

Behind us, in the distance, Eimear's cradle swung in the breeze. Ahead, Brendan, a father she would never know, marched mournfully before his tormentors. Bridget walked close behind him, her head bowed.

They knew his fate, as did the curious eyes that observed from behind the hedgerows. These unfortunate families of landless labourers and travelling crofters lived in the ditches. For shelter, they laid slanted sticks across ditches and drains. A roof was fashioned from branches covered in sods of earth. Everywhere, emaciated children stood - wet, dirty and expressionless. They had no past or future. Their clothes were rags discarded by the big house. The women appeared haggard, the men wild.

The land was coarse and mountainous with hills, valleys and bogs. My feet, unaccustomed to the harsh terrain, were bleeding profusely, but I felt no pain.

The rain cleared and the mist lifted. Up ahead was

Ballinacor House, below dense forests circled by large tracts of bog and marsh. Close to the impressive carved oak entrance gates and ramparts was a row of small, single-roomed cottages. This was the Barony of Ballinacor, "a town near a marsh". Through the half-doors, I could see young girls seated by open fires, some engrossed in needlework, others spinning wool. All were employed by the estate.

A ragged urchin walked up the street pulling a reluctant ox. He was painfully thin with coarse, dark brown hair and alert, hazel-coloured eyes.

A tall, elegant woman in her late thirties walked confidently from the estate with her maid servants. Two enormous Irish wolfhounds bounded along playfully at her heels. Waiting obediently at the perimeter walls were three artisan women dressed in colourful knits.

The woman nodded to Bridget by way of recognition, then summoned the captain, who stood to attention. A handsome man, I thought. Even though he was approaching middle age, his eyes still shone with boyish devilment.

The soldiers, with their prisoner, disappeared through a bank of imposing oak trees close to the main house. Bridget turned to face the woman, her head bowed in respect and self-pity. The woman addressed the soldier.

"Captain Martin, am I to believe that the stories relating to Brendan Burke are indeed true?"

As the woman spoke, she cocked her head to one side in a playful gesture. She was obviously a cunning woman. Her skin was freckled, her complexion ruddy. She had a snub nose and a full, sensuous mouth. Her hair was a wonderful rich auburn colour and cascaded loosely over her narrow shoulders. The heavy, plum-coloured cape worn over a rich, black satin dress, was many sizes too big for her, but did not disguise the slimness of her body. After an exchange of words, she dismissed the captain and turned towards Bridget.

"Madame," Bridget pleaded, "I beseech and pray that you use your influence with the great chieftain to secure a lenient judgement for Brendan." Bridget had chosen her words carefully. She continued, "He is a simple man and cannot be held fully responsible for the inclement weather that has diseased and ravaged the crops. Madame, I beseech you to appeal to the great chieftain for leniency."

"Bridget, it is you who is simple. Brendan is guilty of a far greater crime ... treason. It has been suggested - considered, but never proven - that Brendan has been passing privileged information on the movements of the clan to the Crown forces. Last night, in the Glenmalure Valley, a small party of Crown soldiers were captured. Under interrogation, they advised that Brendan was the main source of their knowledge.

"Bridget, your man has the blood of our kinsfolk on his hands and this day his soul will do battle with those in whom he confided and then condemned. As he chose to live by the Crown, it has been decreed that he will die by her laws also. This afternoon, Bridget, I must inform you that Brendan, for his crimes, will bow his head to the executioner's axe."

Bridget fell to the ground. The three women at the gate ran forward and carried her to one of the cottages.

"You are not known to me. What is your name?" the woman addressed me, haughtily.

"No, madame. I am from Wicklow. My name is Grainne. My mother died in childbirth, my father from old age. I came to the hills to find work. I lost my way and was sheltered by Brendan and Bridget."

"I can see and hear that you are an educated girl. Was your father a man of learning?" the woman queried.

"Yes, madame. He was a scholar."

"Grainne, am I then to assume that you can read and write in English?"

"Yes, madame."

"That is good. My name is Rose. I am mistress of Ballinacor House. Some time ago, the chieftain returned from a raid in Dublin with a collection of books from a gentlemen's library. I thirst for worldly knowledge. Life in the big house during the long winter months can be wearisome. Grainne, you shall be my companion. Make haste to the kitchen and ask for Maud. Tell her the mistress has requested that she find you a comfortable bed, then set a place for you at her table."

I walked slowly up the long, winding driveway. Beyond the oak trees, I came upon a group of thatched mud and stone cottages. Here lived the Gallowglass, the elite band of fearsome mercenary foot soldiers who had arrested Brendan. Ahead was Ballinacor House, a forbidding white-washed stone and timber fortification commanding views of pasture that rolled as far as the eye could see. Here before me grazed enormous herds of cattle, sheep and horses. Below, the Glenmalure valley was a natural amphitheatre, long and narrow with steep sides rising to the sky.

As I nervously entered the kitchen, Maud stood over a young girl basting a side of beef on a spit. She was no more than twenty years old, tall, slender and upright with a pale, clear skin. Her long blond hair was tied with leather thongs and slides. I viewed with interest the vast array of spices, herbs and animals hanging from hooks in the ceiling. There were rabbits, chickens and pheasants. The young, sullen girl reluctantly rotated the spit.

"You are an impudent wench, Mary Ryan, and if you intend to remain in this household, you had better learn some manners. Off with you to the farm manager's cottage and fetch a pail of milk. And be quick."

I introduced myself. Maud regarded me curiously for a moment, then observed with horror my swollen, numbed and bloodied feet. I explained my predicament and that the mistress had employed me as her companion.

"I trust you have better manners than this scurvy beggar," Maud joked.

In the corner, another young girl was making butter. Opposite, a simple boy plucked a chicken. Maud walked across the flagstone floor to a wood stove. She poured liquid from a steaming black pot into a deep wooden bowl, then walked back across the room. Smiling sympathetically, she handed me the bowl. It was a chicken stock with barley. While I devoured the warm broth, Maud washed and applied an ointment to my feet. The warmth of the kitchen and Maud's unexpected kindness were comforting, a single contented moment in a turbulent time.

One hour later, we were ordered from the kitchen and led to the back of the house where the inhabitants of the village had gathered.

Mounted on a stationary, flat wagon were two soldiers and a priest. The three women who had earlier carried Bridget into the cottage were there at the front of the baying crowd, as was the boy who had been dragging the ox. Brendan was led through the crowd, his hands secured behind his back with leather thongs. His head was bloodied and completely shaven. Angry men, women and children moved forward menacingly to strike him. A scuffle broke out. The soldiers drew their swords and raised their pikes.

It was mid-afternoon and an icy wind blew up from the valley below. The tails of Brendan's blood-splattered shirt rustled in the wind.

Observing was Fiach MacHugh, an angry, imposing middle-aged man of over six foot who strode out with the confidence of a chieftain - vigorous in spirit and health. His cloak, which was sleeveless, was secured by a jewelled brooch fastened at the shoulder. He wore trousers that were secured at the waist by a cord. His tooled leather knee-boots were covered in a rich, red fox fur.

They marched to the wagon. Two muscle-bound Gallowglass soldiers lifted Brendan roughly onto the wagon. The crowd parted to allow Fiach MacHugh to mount the platform. Brendan stared impassively at the bloodied block of wood, the axe and the sombre executioner.

"Followers of the clan, you see before you a traitor - a man who, for scant reward, sold the lives of your kinsfolk to the supporters of our fervent enemies, the Crown. This man, who chose to live by the Crown, will today die by its traditions. Let this be a lesson to anyone who betrays their chieftain, Fiach MacHugh."

Fiach MacHugh dismounted and walked to a vantage point on higher ground.

The crowd cheered as the priest came forward to administer the last rites to Brendan. The prayers completed, he hung wooden rosary beads around his neck. Brendan fingered the beads while he searched among the crowd for Bridget.

The executioner came forward and led Brendan to the wooden block. Brendan knelt down. The executioner rolled back his shirt collar and ran the sharp blade across his neck. Brendan shivered. A small trickle of blood appeared. The crowd went silent. I turned away as the axe was raised. Three times I heard the clumsy executioner drop his axe on Brendan's neck. Each time I looked up, his shaven head remained connected to his body.

Brendan struggled and wrestled in pain and fury as four soldiers leaped upon the wagon to hold him secure. I looked to Maud. She smiled. On the fourth mighty stroke, Brendan's head was finally severed from his shoulders in a fountain of blood.

CHAPTER 4

Over the following weeks, I helped Maud cook and clean in the kitchen. She was a cheerful, likeable, hardworking girl and was the nearest I had to a friend. My main function stemmed from my understanding of medicine. Albeit limited in modern times, it was considered extensive in the middle ages.

After dark, I was summoned to the mistress's study to read prose and recite poetry while being warmed by the scented logs in the open fire.

Fiach MacHugh, an obtrusive and arrogant man, suffered from gout, which required a herbalist to be in constant attendance, brewing potions and applying liniments. He paid little attention to the mistress and was concerned that she wished to study and speak the tongue of his enemies. The duties of a mistress, he decreed, were to manage the house and host social visits and clan gatherings.

In contrast to Fiach MacHugh and his wishes, the mistress was a benevolent, even-tempered woman who instructed and supervised the women in the artisan cottages in animal husbandry, weaving and dyeing fabrics.

Fiach MacHugh, the Lord of Glenmalure, never relaxed. He often paced the gallery room, which ran the entire length of the house, for hours planning raids on rival settlements. He was a merciless warrior who, without consideration, murdered men, women and children. He freely plundered and desecrated libraries and churches. While I was in residence, he raided the house of a rival chieftain in Kildare. After selecting and removing the fine antiquities, he ordered that the house be burned with the occupants locked inside. On the return journey, he ordered his men to raid a church in Crumlin, where they even removed the slates from the roof. His pedigree was mean and his sons - Felim, Reamonn and Turlough, also dour quarrelsome men - appeared eager to carry on the family tradition. His daughter Margery, despite the influences of her brothers, was a friendly, dignified girl. Her marriage to Lord Baltinglass was beneficial to the clan due to the close proximity of their estates.

Access to Ballinacor House was limited. Wheeled transport was non-existent. Apart from the wild men and wolves that wandered the hills, the hazardous mountain pathways, inclement weather and highwaymen made travel beyond the perimeter walls dangerous.

When the chieftain and his armies travelled, they took with them their great herds of horses, cattle and sheep. These provided sustenance in milk, beef and mutton and warmth in wool and hides. It was also wise to have their wealth where it could best be watched over. The mercenary Gallowglass soldiers often took their payment in livestock or hides. The labourers who stayed behind tilled the land with oxen. On the O'Byrne estate, they had an unusual, if cruel, method of attaching the plough to the unfortunate animal's tail. The land, which was strewn with rock and oak forests, was set in oats and corn. The Crown forces cut down the oak to use in shipbuilding and to eliminate trees as a form of refuge for rebels and criminals.

Life in the kitchen was generally boring but, on this

particular day, the kitchen was alive with activity. Women from the village had arrived at daybreak. Tonight, Fiach MacHugh and Rose were entertaining another Gaelic clansman from the north of Ireland - Black Hugh O'Donnell. The mistress had invited me to attend. It would be an exciting night. Rhymers, jesters, singers and even a small orchestra had been employed.

The mistress entered the kitchen. Maud was combing my hair. She did this every day with a double-sided wooden comb. One side was for untangling the hair, the other for removing lice. It was midday. Her daughter Margery, visiting from Baltinglass, accompanied her.

"Maud, have you all the food and drink for the feast prepared?"

"Yes, mistress. We have whitebait with chopped pickle, sour cream and onions. The main meal will be of roast venison, mutton and beef with cabbage, onions, leeks and watercress. To finish, fruit, cheese, hazelnuts, olives and the finest of French wine and brandy.

The mistress nodded her approval.

"Black Hugh this day," the mistress continued, "has brought to the house splendid gifts of oriental rugs and silver. It would be mannerly and proper of us to complement our table tonight by displaying these finely carved silver knives, forks and spoons.

"Mother," Margery interrupted, "can Grainne join us this afternoon on the stag hunt?"

The mistress deliberated, then replied, "Yes, of course. It will be most interesting for her."

"Would you like to join us?" Margery enquired.

"Yes, please!" I said excitedly.

"Well, dress warmly and report to my chamber within the hour."

An hour later, I was galloping across a wet, muddy

field with Margery, Fiach, Black Hugh, his followers and over one hundred footmen.

Ahead, a disciplined pack of excited, yelping hounds picked up the scent of a red deer. The frightened animal bounded aimlessly into a stream close to a thicket of gorse. It escaped fortuitously when a fox was disturbed and ran from the scrub. The hounds immediately picked up the scent and gave chase. The hunt master indicated to the footmen with his hunting horn to cut off the fox's escape from the south of the valley. The fox had no alternative but to head west.

We galloped fearlessly across the rugged mountainside, leaping streams, hedges, walls and fallen trees. In the distance I could see the fox, his wild eyes tired and frightened. He stopped and turned to consider his options. The hounds had a clear scent and were closing in.

My horse, Sheanna, was sure-footed and brave. She attacked and cleared stone walls and ditches with an assurance that was inspiring. With growing confidence, I loosened the reins and we raced clear of the stragglers and lodged just behind the master.

The fox, in full view and on open rocky ground, was floundering. While negotiating the damp, slippery rocks leading down a steep incline, he turned instinctively to look over his shoulder. Unfortunately, he missed his footing and tumbled heavily down the side of the hill, falling onto a perilous ledge overhanging the Avonbeg river. He lay motionless.

The horses and the stronger of the hounds were eating up the ground. Stunned, the fox tried to stand up, but his front paw hung limp and broken. He fell forward in shock and pain, almost tumbling headlong onto the razor-sharp rocks hundreds of feet below. Above him, the hounds bayed.

The huntsman, observed by the eager and critical faces of Fiach MacHugh and Black Hugh, ordered a footman to clamber down for the fox's brush. The fox, in shock and fear, watched the man with a curved knife gripped between his teeth ease his way down to the ledge. The fox leaned over and regarded the rocks hundreds of feet below. He raised himself up on his three paws and growled defiantly at his tormentor, then hurled himself into space.

I pulled the warm cape around my shoulders and tucked it under my chin.

After another unsuccessful run, Fiach MacHugh led his hounds and guests to a secluded hollow where his staff had erected tents and prepared a midday meal. Inside the tents, trestle tables were set with mulled wine, ale, cold meats, oat cakes, fruit and cheese. Outside, fires had been lit. Suspended over the flames hung animal hides filled with steaming mutton and vegetables. The cooked meat was served on wooden platters and eaten with the fingers. The chieftains dismounted and removed their embroidered tunics.

A man played the harp while Black Hugh and Fiach MacHugh conversed earnestly. The horses, with bridles of fine-tooled leather and padded, quilted saddles, grazed under the watchful eyes of footmen. A tall, painfully thin, well-spoken man dressed like a clown climbed upon a rock.

"My lords and ladies, I welcome you to the land of the O'Byrne clan and the site of the Battle for Glenmalure.

"Our chieftain, Fiach MacHugh, and his clan have occupied these lands uninterrupted for over three hundred years. In that time, the Crown has mounted many unsuccessful raids, but none as great as that of thirteen years ago when Lord Grey marched his army of one thousand soldiers against Fiach MacHugh.

"The Crown forces approached Ballinacor House.

23

Fiach MacHugh, forewarned, had moved his followers and livestock further up into the mountain mist. Lord Grey followed. Fiach MacHugh lured his enemy to Barravore Ford, then turned and stood his ground. Lord Baltinglass, unknown to Lord Grey, came from behind to cut off the Crown's line of retreat.

"The Crown soldiers were tired and hungry from their long march across the snow-covered Wicklow mountains. Cruelly buffeted by an icy wind, their hands and bodies were numbed from the cold. In disarray, the troops rebelled against their officers.

"In a hail of lead and smoke, the valley echoed to the sound of O'Byrne muskets. In open battle, the musket is a clumsy weapon. But firing at a wall of one thousand confused Crown troops, it was, on this day, most effective.

"The Lord Deputy, his experience bought this day with the price of his soldiers lives, urged his men to face the lance, sword and pike of the marauding O'Byrnes. To the rising sound of warpipes, the O'Byrne clan attacked and won its greatest victory.

"Nine hundred English soldiers died on this mountain of shot, steel and cold. All are buried here as a lasting monument to the power and guile of the O'Byrne clan. Two of their commanding officers are buried over there in Big Man's Grave."

The feasting and storytelling over, the hunters set out again. We followed the hounds until nightfall through forests of great oak and along steep, craggy, granite mountains. The majestic deer and fox had eluded us. Margery commented that Fiach was angered and embarrassed by the failure of his huntsmen and that they would be punished. Of that I was certain.

Back at the house, all the servants moved diligently. There was great excitement. Thousands of candles were lit and the house gleamed in a magical yellow hue. A young Venetian man from the O'Donnell clan sang sweetly while accompanying himself on a harpsichord. The tables were set with elegant dried flowers and exquisite earthenware plates and bowls. The chieftains, surrounded by their obedient servants, drank pitchers of frothy ale and wine before retiring to Fiach MacHugh's chambers to play card games and dice.

Later, the mistress and Fiach MacHugh officially greeted Black Hugh and his guests in the great hall. There were blazing wood fires burning at each end of the hall. On a large oak table there was an array of finely-crafted silver bowls filled with hot spiced punch.

I was escorted by Margery, resplendent in a sapphire taffeta gown embroidered with golden vines with lemon petticoats. Her ebony-coloured hair had been arranged in rolls and curls, rouge applied to her cheeks and lips and her eyebrows darkened with burnt cork. Earlier, I too had endured the ritual of brushing, painting, powdering and tightening of stays. Margery, to my surprise, presented me with an emerald necklace and drop earrings to match my bottle green gown. My hair was piled high and secured with two diamond-clustered hair ties. I felt rather grand, if uneasy.

As we stood behind the excited guests waiting to be formally introduced to Fiach MacHugh and Rose, I reflected on the various experiences I had witnessed over the past weeks. From arriving at Mountclare to start my first term at boarding school, finding the "Key to the Past," moving through the door and arriving in Wicklow in 1916, then meeting the Countess Markievicz and experiencing the horror and futility of the Rising and now my unexpected arrival in 1593 and the shocking spectacle of Brendan's execution. I, of course, missed my family, but I was equally enthralled by these new sights, sounds, smells and experiences.

The introductions completed, we moved with the other one hundred or so guests into the gallery room. The wooden floors and walls were decorated with rich oriental rugs and tapestries presented to Fiach MacHugh by Black Hugh. In the centre of the room, a hideously deformed man had taken up a position on a podium and was preaching to a large attentive audience.

"Three years ago, Sir John Perrot issued orders that the young clansman Red Hugh, son of Black Hugh O'Donnell, should be kidnapped. The Crown's agents carried out this deed on Lough Swilly. They lured the boy and his two young companions aboard a sailing ship. After plying them with the finest French wine, they bound and trussed them then set sail for Dublin Castle.

"To this day, Red Hugh remains malnourished and close to death in the dank, chilled darkness of a stone cell in the Bermingham Tower of Dublin Castle."

"An astute rhymer and well versed too," whispered Margery.

"His reputation in raising support for his master, Black Hugh, is well recorded. He is an important man, second only to the chieftain himself. He travels the length and breadth of Europe and, through his knowledge and satires, has the ability to advise and incite war and rebellion. His attendance tonight is to gather support for a proposed expedition to Dublin to release young Red Hugh from Dublin Castle."

Three pipers entered the elegantly furnished gallery room and piped the guests to the dining room. The feast was splendid and, even though the finest of silver cutlery and goblets were supplied, most of the guests, through force of habit, used their hands. A young woman in a frumpish, grey taffeta dress and lace cap played the harp.

She could have been considered beautiful except she was bloated and flushed by pregnancy. The tables were, as expected, laden with food and drink that flowed stronger than the Avonbeg river. Within a short time, the controlled social gathering became quite boisterous.

The mistress, as always, monitoring proceedings, clapped her hands. A tall, handsome Romany with large gold earrings entered the room and struck up a polka on the violin. He was closely followed by a group of six colourfully dressed dancing gypsy girls. They skipped and pirouetted majestically while banging and crashing copper tambourines festooned with red streamers.

As the girls were dancing, the mistress passed back into the gallery room where a larger group of musicians were setting up their instruments. The dancing completed, the gypsy girls disappeared and the guests were ushered back into the gallery room where the small orchestra had begun to play. The oriental rugs had been rolled back and the exposed wooden floorboards creaked as the joyous gathering danced up and down the floor in running, sliding steps.

Margery, the mistress and I remained in the banqueting hall, but moved to a smaller gate-legged card table.

"How about a game of cards?" Margery enquired.

"Oh yes, that is a wonderful idea. How about a game of Gleek?'" the mistress suggested.

Margery and I nodded our approval. The mistress summoned two servants. She instructed one to fetch a set of cards from her study, the other a cool earthenware jug of French red wine. When the servants returned, the mistress dealt each of us twelve cards, leaving the remaining cards in the centre of the table. Margery poured the wine as the mistress explained the rules of the game. The idea was to collect three cards of the one suit. The winner was the player with no cards left.

We had been playing and drinking wine for almost an hour when a group of the O'Donnell clan, led by the rhymer, interrupted and suggested that we should elect a King and Queen. It was an old Roman practice and customary in the north of Ireland at clan gatherings. The mistress thought it was a great idea and, within minutes, a huge fruit cake was ceremoniously carried into the hall by two footmen. The servants cut and handed everyone a slice of cake.

"Go on, Grainne," said Margery. "If you find a dried pea in the cake you will be the Queen."

Over in the corner, a handsome young man, his sea-blue eyes full of zest and mischief, jumped to his feet, a single dried pea held aloft. Beside me, Margery smiled as she gripped the other pea in triumph between her teeth.

"My lords and ladies," the rhymer exclaimed. "I present to you the King and Queen of Ballinacor. More handsome a match has not been made in heaven."

As the gathering cheered, the banqueting door was thrown open and four servants carried two ornate golden chairs to the top of the hall, placing them on a raised podium. The rhymer invited the King and Queen to take their places.

Margery, her eyes fired with excitement, walked regally to the throne while the younger man was carried shoulder high by his inebriated friends. Red velvet robes were placed over their Royal shoulders and mock brass crowns on their heads. Sceptres encrusted with paste jewels were laid at their feet. The young King rose and, banging his sceptre on the podium, requested silence.

"As your King, I decree that the orchestra should move this instant from the sanctuary of the house and continue to enchant us with their melodic strains in the falling snow."

Within minutes, the hall had cleared and the drunken revellers could be seen and heard dancing joyously and with great difficulty in the snow.

The rhymer, his frail misshapen body framed in the carved oak portal, spoke.

"Madame, allow me to introduce myself."

His face was pointed and resembled an otter. While he spoke, he self-consciously fingered the faded silk ruffles circling his wrinkled neck. The three middle fingers of his right hand were fused into one and curled inwards like a hook.

"I am Graham of the Highlands - Scottish by birth, Irish by choice."

Graham threw back his coat-tails and sat down.

"I suspect, madame, by your demeanour that you are a card player comparable to the infamous Pirate Queen. It seems that the Gaelic woman is as deft and cunning a player of cards as she is of men.

"Your chieftain, sir, speaks highly of this Pirate Queen of Clew Bay. Is she as brave and notorious as the great stories relate?" the mistress enquired.

Graham stood, raised up his twisted torso, and recited in his soft Scottish accent:

An old grey tower, where storms and sea waves beat,
Perched upon a rocky cliff beneath a yawning tide,
　　a lofty cavern, a fine retreat,
For pirates galleys and their treasures she will greet,
A hundred steps lead upwards to a lonely chamber.
Bold and brave are those who climb these stairs,
　　slippery from the wave.
Grace O'Malley the commander in chief of a band of
　　thieves and murderers to meet.

"For centuries," he continued, "the O'Malley clan have sailed perilous sea routes, fishing and trading with Ulster, Scotland, Spain, Portugal and France. Grace O'Malley is leader of the clan and a legendary sea captain. Despite her advanced years and her gender, she carries the proud tradition of her father.

"In galleys powered by wind and oar, they export hides, salted fish, linen and butter while importing wines, rich silks, tapestries and spice. It requires much skill, knowledge and bravery to navigate a safe passage on these trade routes. The weather conditions are unpredictable and at times ferocious.

"I am proud to relate that, two summers past, I was invited to sail on her merchant galley, the Maid of Clew, on a trade mission. Our destination was the Portuguese port of Lisboa. As we passed Mizen, we were ambushed by a Turkish pirate ship. When the Maid of Clew appeared to be lost, Grace O'Malley came on deck and led her men to a famous victory through example and bravery.

"Today, she may be advanced in years, but not in mind and body. She stands tall, dark, robust and proud with unique qualities of leadership. She is, despite these qualities, the most feminine of women who demands respect, obedience and loyalty.

"Grace O'Malley has amassed a great knowledge and understanding of an unpredictable sea that is both a fickle friend and a dangerous ally. It is certainly a remarkable woman that can stand alone and survive the dangerous waters of the west coast of this island for close to forty years.

"With parties of up to five hundred fighting men and twenty galleys, she burns, plunders and raids the rich coastal estates, returning triumphant to the sanctuary of her castle, Rockfleet, in Clew Bay. The castle affords a natural protection, perched high on a cliff. From its battlements, there is an uninterrupted view to the distant horizon. There are hundreds of small islands, underwater rocks and reefs that render Rockfleet inaccessible to all but the experienced sailors, who have mapped its treacherous waters. It is here that Grace O'Malley has amassed her fortune, raiding the larger, less agile Spanish and English galleys. Her versatile and speedy ships swoop out from the cover of the islands around the bay to attack faltering merchant ships. Her seafaring warriors board the captured galley and, depending on the cargo, plunder or pilot the vessel a safe passage for a consideration."

Graham again broke into verse.

She stood alone her fair skin battered by a salted breeze,
Firmly commanding her oarsmen and her galleys,
And where the bending strand and rock and ocean wrestle,
Between the sea and the land, she built her castle.

One day as dawn broke a Spanish merchant ship came sailing by,
For Galway port with gold and fine wines she was heading.
Behind him a merciless storm of rain and thunder,
Before him Grace O'Malley with a cannoned galley in search of plunder.

Grace O'Malley has, over the years, built up great wealth from her raids on land and sea. She has suffered many setbacks, too, none worse than from the ruthless Sir Richard Bingham, governor of Connaught elected by the Queen of England. Sir Richard has in the past imprisoned

Grace O'Malley and unlawfully confiscated great tracts of her valuable land and livestock. He also ordered his brother, Captain John Bingham, to lay siege on the fertile lands belonging to her son Owen. Not content, he also seized Owen's herd of over four thousand cattle and five hundred stud mares. In the course of this duty, John Bingham also saw fit to round up and hang eighteen of Owen's followers. The ensuing day, Bingham concluded his outrageous assault by conniving to have Owen murdered on the pretext that he was attempting to escape.

"In order to secure Grace O'Malley's good behaviour, Tibbot, another son, is being held hostage in the household of the same John Bingham. Donal, her brother, is in gaol. His crime was being in the company of men that were suspected of murdering soldiers.

"To conclude, Grace O'Malley is eager to safeguard her position as Queen of Connaught and has pleaded a voluntary submission to the Queen of England. She is a nurse to all rebellions, but mindful of growing English influence in Connaught. Bingham has robbed her of a livelihood. Her future is bleak. Her fleet no longer dominates the western coastline or sails in defiance and piracy. She seeks not to regain her former standing, but to re-establish her existence. The only recourse open to her is to appeal to the highest authority ... the Queen of England. Grace O'Malley, it is reported, has written to Elizabeth requesting the right to invade with the sword and gun all the enemies of the Crown."

"Some, I hear, call her Granuaile. How did she get this name?" the mistress enquired.

"As a child, Grace O'Malley accompanied her father on many of his long voyages and learned to navigate and sail. This, to Grace, was preferable to helping her mother in the castle. A great confrontation occurred one day when her father, on her mother's insistence, declined to take Grace on a voyage. Her mother did not approve of her young daughter travelling the seas with such ill-bred men. Grace responded by vanishing to her chamber only to return shortly with her head shaven and dressed in her brother's clothes. Her brother laughed and called her Granuaile. Bald Grace."

"Tell me, Graham, what plans have been laid to rescue young Red Hugh from Dublin Castle?"

"Provisions have been made for the privy hole in Red Hugh's cell in Dublin Castle to be left open. This will allow Hugh and the two O'Neill boys, Arthur and Henry, to follow the human excrement from the privy hole in the tower to the River Liffey. The Earl of Tyrone has arranged for his foster brothers, the O'Hagan's, to help release the prisoners. The Crown's forces will expect them to run for Ulster. But, with the help of the O'Byrne clan, they intend to guide them to Glenmalure."

I was tired. My eyes were heavy with wine and smoke. I could hear the revellers returning. I excused myself and headed for my bedchamber. Secure in the room, I undressed and spent time at the window watching the cattle and horses huddled together, sheltering from the blinding snow.

CHAPTER 5

The next morning, I entered the kitchen as dawn broke over the crisp white landscape. Apart from Maud and myself, the only other person in the kitchen was a soundly sleeping member of the visiting O'Donnell clan.

"Poor child," Maud said, looking in the direction of a young girl curled on a sheepskin rug close to the range. She lay in the foetal position, a fringed shawl pulled around her bony shoulders. She was covered in ash and soot.

"An overabundance of French wine no doubt," Maud remarked. "I would not wish to have her head when she wakes."

Maud served up a fine breakfast of hot oat porridge, flap jacks, bread, butter and milk flavoured with honey. We were in deep conversation when the kitchen door opened. The mistress stood framed in the doorway, her appearance unkempt, her eyes clouded.

"Grainne, I am glad I found you! This morning the chieftain ordered that, with your knowledge of medicine, you must accompany the Gallowglass on their march to Dublin. You are to be an aid to the travelling physician.

"Maud, I am assigning you the responsibility of ensuring that Grainne is warmed in body and soul. You may select suitable clothes and footwear from the women in the cottages. Make sure that Grainne has a change of clothes. The weather on the mountain will be hostile."

The mistress handed me a small mahogany box inlaid with brass. Inside the box was a hunting knife.

"It belonged to my father," the mistress explained. "You may need it!"

The mistress embraced me warmly, turned and left the kitchen. Her sweet perfume still hung in the air as Maud put on her heavy woollen cloak and fur-covered boots and disappeared into the deep snow piled high at the back door.

The girl at the fireplace stretched out and groaned softly. In shock, she opened her eyes. Bemused, she looked all around the kitchen. Reassured, she frowned, rubbed her forehead and fell asleep again. I went over and pulled the cloak around her shoulders. Her copper hair was as thick as a man's wrist and hung in a pony tail reaching to the small of her back. Tiny wisps of hair tickled her rose-coloured cheeks.

The back door opened. A cold breeze circled the kitchen. Captain Martin's sturdy frame stood silhouetted in the doorway. Surprisingly, he was not dressed as a soldier but as an itinerant. He wore a cocked hat trimmed with braid. His long, coarse-cropped hair sat on the frayed velvet collar of his rust-coloured coat. Behind him, the Gallowglass soldiers were similarly dressed.

"The chieftain informs me that you are to accompany us to Dublin on our mission to lead Red Hugh to freedom. Make ready. We depart from the main gates within the hour."

Captain Martin turned and ordered his men to load sufficient provisions on the horses.

An hour later, I stood with Maud at the gates. It was colder than I had ever thought possible. The mountain was silent as man and beast sheltered against the formidable elements. Smoke from the artisan cottages billowed upwards towards patches of vivid blue sky. The oak trees below in the valley were in a frozen solitude. Upon the crisp air floated a gentle breeze that cut and stung my cheeks. Threatening grey clouds now appeared in the sky. Their unusual colour bothered me. It began to snow again.

I removed my goatskin gloves, tightened the belt on my thick, saffron-coloured wool cape and tucked the coarse woollen leggings into my fur-lined leather boots. The itinerant tailors, Maud told me, dyed all their clothes with mixtures of saffron as it was thought to have anti-lice properties.

Captain Martin and his company of twenty men re-appeared marching through the deep, powdered snow. They were dressed as a nomadic band of artisans. The soldiers halted at the gates, large flakes of snow settling on their shoulders. The captain approached the gates with a young man. His hair was fair and tied up with a faded yellow ribbon. His shoulders were broad and seemed to strain at the seams of his woollen cloak. As he extended his hand, I noticed his bony wrists and long, slender, aristocratic fingers. His smile was friendly and without malice. His thin nose was set between large, heavy-lidded grey eyes.

"Miss Grainne, may I present James McKinnon, our travelling physician."

"I am delighted to meet you. I am informed that you are a learned young woman with a knowledge of medicine," James mocked as he spoke in English.

"My father, sir, was an eminent man of learning whose studies included medicine. My knowledge is of a passive nature and not as a result of extensive study," I replied.

Captain Martin called his men into line. The long march to Dublin began.

I walked next to James. He was a mildly affected

young man who had something to say about everything, little of which made sense. He lived in London, in a place called Spitalfields, and was an only child. His mother ran a tavern called the Royal Oak. When James was eighteen, his father, a fleet admiral, was reported lost fighting the Spanish Armada off the west coast of Ireland. They lived at the time in an imposing house belonging to the admiralty in Portsmouth. The house overlooked the fleet in the wide bay below.

Five years on, the house reverted back to the admiralty and the Crown pension ceased. The admiral's body was never found and, thus, his mother fell on hard times trying to put James through medical school. She moved back to London to be near James and, with what little money she had left, purchased the Royal Oak. James had travelled to Ireland to obtain written confirmation of his father's death.

We marched on in silence.

"On a march," James now informed me, "talking employs oxygen and ultimately tires the body."

We came upon a wooden bridge which precariously spanned the foaming and swiftly rising Avonbeg river. It was constructed from pine trees crudely roped together. We had been marching now for over two hours. Looking back up the valley, I imagined that this bleak but beautiful landscape enveloped in a threatening grey mist was almost primeval. This was how the world must have been before it was inhabited by man.

I felt uneasy. James acknowledged my discomfort. We headed on to Laragh. The wind began to rise rapidly as we climbed, its hollow roar swelling into a fearsome thunder. The horses became anxious. The Gallowglass soldiers showed no emotion; they just bowed their heads and leaned into the freezing wind and snow that had begun to fall again.

The track circling the mountain narrowed and began to move under foot. Captain Martin ordered that we should be linked by a safety rope. We moved on. I was third in line behind the captain and James.

The lakes at Roundwood appeared below. I was frozen. My hands and feet were numb. and swollen. It began to hail. I was wet through. My clothes clung to my skin. The rough woollen leggings had frozen into tiny balls of ice. My lips began to crack and bleed. I searched the faces of my fellow travellers looking for weakness … nothing. The Gallowglass were a rugged bunch of men, chosen for their gallantry in battle, not conversation. They advanced through the blinding snow in silence, their obedient horses following through this menacing, but dazzling, world.

Every step, every yard gained on the mountain was now at such an expense that the effort left me trembling and faint with hunger.

Captain Martin stopped on a wide ledge and ushered his men around him. Shouting through the howling wind, he explained that they could not shelter and, in order to prevent frostbite and, ultimately, loss of life, they must at all costs keep moving.

"It is, I estimate, a one hour march to Enniskerry. We will rest and take sustenance there," he roared.

The wind began to swirl. I looked up. A gigantic wall of snow towered above us. The slope was so steep and the snow so abundant that it no longer held firm and began to slide in waves, starting small avalanches. The drift increased in size and speed. All at once, I was tumbling backwards into a deep ravine. The rope around my waist took up the slack and tightened. I began to spin round and round on the rope like a puppet. The motion tightened the rope and it wound around my neck. I began to choke. I had no choice. In an instant, I pulled out the hunting knife the mistress had given me earlier. Thankfully, the serrated blade sliced through the rope with ease.

Released from a life-line that was strangling me, I fell back again into a void. Thankfully, the deep snow of a wider ledge below cushioned my fall. I lay there bewildered, my head aching. Before I had time to gather my senses, I was enveloped in another avalanche. I was buried deep in the snow, the weight of which was crushing me. I moved my two arms to my chest and, in doing so, made a small space which allowed me to expand my lungs and breathe. I began to panic and made desperate attempts to push back the snow. I could not move. I was buried in a groaning, unstable snow coffin mindful that at any second I could be hurtled further down the steep mountain.

I lay stretched out, a blind panic welling through my body. Above me, I could hear the faint sound of the storm howling. I was fraught with terror. I knew I must remain calm. It was a struggle of mind over matter. I tried to move my toes ... nothing. I considered death for the first time. My whole being revolted against the idea and I convinced myself that it was only a matter of time before I was rescued. But could I hold out long enough?

My mind wandered. There was a deathly silence. I tried to create another air pocket. The weight of the snow was pressing hard against my chest. I moved my arms upwards, again trying to relieve the pressure from my chest. The reality, like the wet snow seeping through my clothes, was that I was buried alive.

I started to wonder how long it would take before I would finally suffocate and die. Or would it be exposure? I was plunged into an inexplicable stupor. I struggled again, frantically but hopelessly, trying to exhume myself.

I thought I could hear voices above. The blunt end of a pike came through the snow and lodged painfully in my chest. I reached out and grabbed the wooden pole as it was extracted. I called out. Snow fell into my open mouth and I nearly choked. I listened. Within minutes I could feel the weight of the snow lift and then, to my relief, the face of Captain Martin appeared. I had survived.

He stood back and allowed the soldiers to dig me out. I had almost been devoured by the snow and had no feeling whatsoever in my feet or hands. My nose and ears stung. My joints were locked and I could not walk.

I was attached to another rope and roughly hauled back up the snow-covered rock face. James looked alarmingly anxious. He immediately set about stimulating my frozen and static blood supply. Firstly, he sat me upon a back-pack then removed my boots, which now formed a solid lump of ice. My socks and leggings followed. My feet were blue and very badly swollen. He began to massage herb oils into my feet. I felt nothing. He looked concerned. To my astonishment, he ordered two burly soldiers to restrain me. Then picking up the end of a piece of rope he began to roughly flog my hands, feet and toes. My feet I could see were badly blistered. The pain was hideous, but suffering as I was from exposure, fatigue and hunger, I was incapable of resistance. After awhile, I sensed a vague warm feeling. The circulation was returning.

"Stand up, Grainne, and listen carefully to what I am about to say."

I eased myself up with great difficulty. My joints ached and my back was locked. As I stood, it seemed that my toes and feet were absent and that I was walking on stilts. I fell over. James's smiling helped me to my feet.

"Grainne, it is imperative that at all times you keep moving. Even as you walk you must rub your hands and move your toes. You are fortunate. Your heart is strong and your blood rich"

We moved on, leaning hard into the driving snow. The wind continued to howl. I began to tire. I had eaten nothing since early morning my reserves of energy were proving insufficient. Finally, a finger pointed. Below, through the mist, the village of Enniskerry was visible. It was still intensely cold. The mountain had become glassy.

There was a sharp tug from behind on the rope. I nearly lost my footing. My heart stopped. I looked around. The mist was so thick that I could hardly see the soldier walking six feet behind. The mist, snowflakes and thick carpet of snow merged to confuse my vision. The captain and James went back to investigate. I stood morose, bracing myself against the savage wind that continued to cut through my very being. I jumped from foot to foot trying to keep my circulation going. James and the captain appeared out of the mist. We marched on. We were now moving down a sharp incline towards the village.

On the outskirts, we were met by a thick-set man. The wind had dropped, but the snow still fell in large flakes. There was considerably less snow in Enniskerry than on the exposed mountain. We no longer had to physically extract our feet from the deep snow with each labouring step.

It was early afternoon. My spirits rose, albeit moderately. We had been exposed to the mountain for nearly five hours now and, while I welcomed the respite ahead, I greatly feared the continuing march to Dublin.

The man led us up a narrow track to a small stone forge formed in the shape of a horseshoe. The building backed into the side of a hill and was sheltered by a semi-circular belt of pine trees. The horses were led to the stables. A gloved hand opened a small door to the side of the forge. A bank of flickering candles illuminated a dirt floor covered in hoof filings. The rough-cut stone wall weeped with condensation. In the corner was a brazier. I fell to my knees, eased back on my heels and basked in the warm glow from the fire. I removed my boots and inspected my feet. They were inflamed, blistered and sore, but the blood was circulating. My lips were hard and cracked, my nose and ears raw.

The door opened again and a cold wind cut through the atmosphere. A soldier on crutches was manoeuvred through the narrow opening. His face was grim. He was led to some cow hides spread on the dirt floor close to the fire. His facial expression was blank. He lay back and stared at the ceiling with a distinct resignation.

Two Gallowglass soldiers moved to his head. Another handed him a pewter medicine container. The injured man drank the contents. Then, suspending the vessel over his mouth, he waited for the last morsel of medicine to drip onto his tongue.

James eased through the curious soldiers and placed his medical bag on the floor at his feet. Then he knelt and, with a hunting knife, deftly cut off the man's boots. He turned and spoke to me.

"Grainne, take this herbal potion and massage this unfortunate man's hands and feet."

James handed me a clean piece of muslin and a corked medicine jar from his bag. I looked at the man's bulbous, blistered and ruptured feet, oozing with foul-looking puss. I poured some oil on the cloth. I became quite nauseated. I looked away as I massaged his ravaged limbs. Resigned to his destiny, the man continued to stare blankly at the bare wooden beams above his head. James returned and knelt down beside me. He gently inspected the man's lifeless hands, then raised up his right leg and placed it on his lap. He inspected the injured limbs thoroughly. Concerned, he began flicking the man's fingers and toes, trying to stimulate blood flow. Removing a scissors from his medical

42

bag, he began trimming away dead frostbitten tissue. The patient never flinched. He felt nothing.

"I am sorry, Henry," James spoke quietly. "Frostbite has set in and withered your limbs. The toes of your left foot, the fingers of your right hand and your right foot will have to be amputated."

The patient never uttered a word, just nodded and continued to stare blankly at the ceiling. James placed his hunting knife and a small hand saw in the brazier. I continued to massage Henry's feet.

A few minutes later, James removed the knife from the brazier. I stared in disbelief. He took a piece of cold charcoal and drew a ring around the man's pale, white skin just below his ankle. The skin sizzled when the red hot blade of the knife cut through the dead tissue. There was no blood. The hardened, withered skin fell away easily from the bone. I was mesmerised. A soldier handed James the hand saw from the fire. James placed a leather gag in the patient's mouth and the blade on the bone, then began to saw. I stood up and walked to the door as hot tar was painted on the stump to seal the wound and prevent it from bleeding when the circulation returned.

As the church bells in the distance announced mid-afternoon, Captain Martin ordered his men to fetch the horses and make ready to continue the march to Dublin. Fed on salted beef, oat cakes and a hot broth, and with Henry sleeping soundly in the corner, we headed out into what was left of the daylight.

Roped securely together, we followed a track from Enniskerry up into the inhospitable mountain. Soon the damp, chilling mist closed around us. The icy wind that had been restrained by the surrounding hills began to gather momentum and set about attacking my blistered ears, nose and cheeks.

43

With night falling rapidly, we marched on. It began to snow, slowly at first. Within minutes, it became a blinding blizzard. My legs, head and back began to ache again. I was so overcome with exhaustion that I no longer looked where I was going. At times, I selfishly allowed James to pull me along. Dark now, we marched up and up into the clouds then down again into the rocky valleys. My boots were frozen again into two painful, solid blocks of ice. The snow was now almost two feet deep and blowing directly into our faces. I followed blindly up narrow mountain paths. I entered a world of my own, a world that had successfully blocked out the hardship and misery.

Finally we came upon a belt of pine trees lining a small mountain stream. Below was Dublin. We sheltered while the Gallowglass soldiers dug holes in the snow and buried the supplies.

As we arrived on the outskirts of Dublin, the snow abated. Captain Martin called James and me to one side. He spoke directly and officiously.

"The Chieftain Fiach MacHugh has ordered that, on reaching the city walls close to St Patrick's Cathedral, I should allow the physician and Miss Grainne to pass through the gates alone. You will inform the soldiers at the first tower gate that you are a visiting physician. At the second, you will repeat this story, but add that you will be returning within the hour with a patient who is being moved to Bishop's Palace in order to recuperate . You will make directly for Dublin Castle where you will be met at the wooden foot bridge close to the Bermingham Tower. The O'Hagan brothers will deliver to you the young Red Hugh. With him will be fellow prisoners, the O'Neill brothers, Arthur and Henry. You will immediately retrace your steps and exit the city. Before you reach the towers, you must divide. James, you and Henry will escort Red

Hugh as your patient bound for the Bishop's Palace. Grainne, you will pass through as Art's wife. When the Crown's forces realise that Red Hugh has fled, they will expect him to run for Ulster. It is our duty to carry him to Glenmalure."

In New Street, in view of St Patrick's Cathedral, the Gallowglass soldiers retreated and allowed James and me to approach the city alone. There were many varied houses outside the walls, mostly labourers' cottages. Two cows scratched through the snow, trying to graze on the frozen grass below. A small herd of goats huddled together for warmth beneath the high walls surrounding the Cathedral.

James hammered on the gates with his fist. Two Crown soldiers appeared, clearly agitated that anyone should wish to enter the city at this time and in this weather. One of them wiped his wet nose on his sleeve and demanded,

"Where are you heading, sir. Can you not find lodgings across the street and enter the city in the morning?"

"I am a physician from London," replied James," summoned to attend a sick merchant in the city. The inclement weather forced the Queen's galley to port earlier this day in Wicklow. I can assure you, sir, I do not stand at these formidable gates at this moment by choice!"

The gates were opened and we passed through into St. Brendan Street. To the right, inside its walled fortification, was the splendid cathedral, its spire iced in snow. On the elevated west tower, a clock struck nine. The bells tolled in the largest ringing peal I had ever heard. As it diminished, I could clearly hear the heavenly sound of the giant organ and choir within. Ahead was another imposing tower gate.

All along the narrow streets were single-storey labourers' cottages. Candles flickered in the windows, illuminating whole families sitting around open fires. Few ventured out on the snow-covered streets. Those who did were mostly dogs and beggars.

The street was silent. At the second tower gate, we were surveyed by an armed battalion of horse soldiers preparing to depart on their nightly tour of duty. James related his story to the soldiers at the gate, but added that he would be transporting his patient within the hour to the Bishop's Palace. The gates creaked open and we entered St. Nicholas Street.

The houses here were clearly more substantial. They belonged to wealthy merchants and were elaborately constructed with stone and wood. Each barred window reflected the troubled and unruly times. The streets were narrow and cobbled. On each corner, powdered women of the street plied their trade while young and old ragged beggars slept in doorways. The stench of the open sewers was unbearable. Everywhere, taverns were filled to capacity. Dublin was a city of stark contrasts of rich and poor.

Ahead was the Tholsel, or City Hall. A group of angry people were gathered outside. A man stood on a wooden box roaring obscenities against Queen Elizabeth and the prices she offered for exported corn.

We turned right into Skinner's Row. Ahead, we saw the curved arches and delicately carved stonework of Christchurch Cathedral. Beyond lay the fortified walls of Dublin Castle.

I was becoming anxious. We walked past the drawbridge and portcullis and around the castle wall to the footbridge close to the Bermingham Tower. Here we were to meet the O'Hagan brothers. We crossed the small wooden bridge that spanned a tributary of the Liffey and waited. In the distance, a tall, athletic man appeared from the shadows and walked towards us. He was dressed in a black cape, his nose and mouth obscured by a red silk scarf.

"Are you the physician?" the man enquired nervously.

"Yes," replied James.

"Stay here!"

Without a word, the man turned and disappeared into the darkness. James, for the first time, looked nervous. He pulled his cape around his shoulders and under his chin, then began to pace up and down.

There was a noise from under the bridge. James swung around. My legs became weak. A young, barefooted man, wet and dishevelled, walked from the freezing river. He had a youthful face that had prematurely aged. His bright red beard and curled hair was crudely cropped. He looked like an nervous animal. He just stood there. Two other men followed. The first was a sickly young man with vacant eyes. The other clearly his brother with similar features, but with a stronger frame and mad, penetrative eyes.

They stood a moment on the bank. The stench from their clothes was intolerable - not at all surprising as they had escaped through the castle's primitive sewage system.

We immediately retraced our steps, James and I leading the way down Skinners Row, past Christchurch, the Tholsel and into St. Nicholas Street. As we passed a tavern on the corner of Back Lane, a group of men fell out the door into the street. One of them knocked Red Hugh to the ground. Without thinking, Red Hugh jumped to his feet and challenged the man. The man turned to his accomplices and laughed.

"Away with you, you scurvy beggar. I shall not wrestle with a young sewer rat, but I could easily run you through with my sword."

His drunken friends gathered round. One of them, curious, walked from the shadows towards Red Hugh. To my horror, I realised that he was a soldier.

"This is no scurvy beggar. It is Red Hugh O'Donnell."

At that moment, Red Hugh turned and ran. Arthur, Henry, James and I followed. As I ran, my leather boots slid on the iced cobbles. Behind me, I could hear the muffled sound of a horse galloping. The next thing I knew, I was struck across the back of the head with a hard blunt instrument. As I fell to the ground, a horse's hoof brushed against my ear.

CHAPTER 6

I awoke face down on a cold, stone floor. A dull ache filled my head. It was dark. With great difficulty, I raised myself up. A narrow beam of light filtered under the door. I stood and observed the dreary damp hovel that imprisoned me. Above my head was a barred window. A cold north wind blew through the opening. This was Dublin Castle. My eyes adjusted to the dark and I walked across to the door. It must have been over a twelve inches thick and was bolted and locked. My head began to throb. I squinted through the keyhole. I could see nothing, but I could clearly hear a man whimpering like a child. I turned to face the window. Loose rushes were scattered on the flagstone floor. In the corner was a straw pallet.

I lay on the damp straw in a stupor, watching the dawn rise through a small gap in the window close to the ceiling. Outside, the wind whistled as the rain beat incessantly against the castellated walls. The smell of urine was vile. I knew within every nerve in my body that I was in grave danger of being hung for treason. To my horror, I became aware of rats scratching around my feet looking for food. Outside, I could hear footsteps echoing in the stone corridor. I sat up. The footsteps halted outside my cell. A key was placed in the lock. The key turned. Heavy bolts were pulled back. The door opened. It was the gaoler. He was a rugged man with a pointed toothless face. He wore a hare's foot charm on a thick silver chain around his neck.

"Don't worry, young lady. You haven't long to wait. For the crime of treason you will soon kneel before the executioner's block. Your pretty head will be mounted on the castle wall and your body sold to the hospital mortuary for the pursuance of medical science."

The gaoler, with a laugh, closed and bolted the door. I was plunged once again into semi-darkness. Not long after, the door opened again. This time, the gaoler stood back and allowed two soldiers to pass.

"We are ordered by the Lord Chief Justice to deliver you to the Queen's Court."

We walked through a labyrinth of corridors to the grim court room. A foul-smelling gaoler opened the door. Before me, seated in ornately-carved wooden pews, were the soldiers who had been drinking in the tavern the previous night. I flexed my quivering muscles and climbed up into a pulpit-like witness box.

An elderly court clerk dressed in colourful ceremonial robes entered the court from my right. He stood and pounded his mace on the wooden floor.

"Pray stand for the Lord Chief Justice."

The court was silent. The Lord Chief Justice, a self-made man who despised the aristocracy and Papists, entered the court. He was a thin, angry-looking man with jowls that lay in folds on his starched collar.

He gathered his papers. The trial began. The court clerk bowed and introduced the jury. Among them were a butcher, a merchant and two physicians, all of them loyal and pampered servants of the Crown. The Lord Chief Justice turned to the court clerk.

"What hideous crime is the accused charged with?"

"The accused, your honour, is charged with high treason. Last night, under the cover of darkness, she orchestrated the escape of Red Hugh O'Donnell and his followers from the hallowed walls of Dublin Castle."

"Counsel for the accused, how does the prisoner plead?"

A young, fresh-faced man stood, bowed and, regarding me with obvious disdain, replied,

"For the record, your honour, the accused pleads not guilty."

"State your defence, sir!" the Lord Chief Justice retorted impatiently.

My counsel walked towards the bench.

"The accused, your honour, claims to be merely an associate and not the instigator of this heinous crime."

"What then is the prosecution's case?" the Lord Chief Justice enquired.

The Attorney-General, a small wimpish man, walked towards the jury.

"Gentlemen of the jury, before you stands a child of Satan - an angelic face with a heart that beats with the blood of the devil. Listen not to her lies and deceit, but bear witness to the facts. This evil woman crawled willingly through the sewers of this fine city to free a malicious enemy of the Crown. This man, known as Red Hugh, and his wicked accomplices are now free once again to rape, murder and pillage the good citizens of Ireland. I call, my Lord, as my first witness the Captain of the Guard."

The Captain of the Guard bore witness to the skirmish outside the tavern and saw me run with the escaping prisoners. I began to tremble. I had to find a way out. Maybe if I could ...

"Will the witness stand."

The Lord Chief Justice spoke directly to me.

"Have you anything to say in your defence before I address the jury?"

"My Lord," I stuttered. "I only arrived in Dublin this week with my brother, a physician from London. He was summoned from London to attend an ailing merchant. I know nothing of this Red ..."

"I deduce, young lady, that you have, of your own free will, chosen to align with these barbaric Irish men."

The Lord Chief Justice turned to the jury. His direction was so plain and barbed that the foreman returned within minutes with their verdict ...

"Guilty as charged, your honour."

The Lord Chief Justice stood.

"It is incumbent upon me to sentence you to death. The unanimous verdict of the jury is that you are guilty as charged. I will, however, show some mercy and allow you to be imprisoned and put to death in the city of your birth. You will be transported this day to the Tower of London. At the gaoler's pleasure, you will be taken from the Tower to your place of execution, where you will be hanged by the neck, but not until you are dead. For you will be cut down alive, then your bowels must be taken from your body and burnt before your face. Your body will then be divided into four quarters. This spectacle will provide the loyal subjects of the Queen with the opportunity to bear witness to how those guilty of high treason are dealt with by the Crown Courts in Dublin ... May God have mercy on your evil soul."

My legs buckled at the knees and the dusty wooden floor rose up to meet me. My head crashed against the side of the witness box. I passed out.

I came to in the back of an enclosed horse-drawn carriage. I was being tossed from side to side like a rag doll. I tried to move my legs. They were in chains. I clung to the

52

side of the carriage as it rattled and raced over the cobbled streets. The carriage stopped. The door opened. Daylight and a cold sea breeze washed over me. I was temporarily blinded. A hand reached in, grabbed my ankle and pulled me from the carriage. As I was about to hit the ground, another muscular arm grabbed my hand. My head crashed against the side of the carriage.

I could clearly hear water lapping against a pier. I was pulled savagely to my feet. Behind me, men laughed. I was on a busy quay side. Before me was an enormous English wooden warship, its figurehead a majestic carved swordfish. Towering above the main body of the ship and reaching up into the grey sky were three giant masts: fore, main and mizzen. The masts supported the yards, large horizontal poles from which the sails hung. Hundreds of ropes controlled the sails and supported the masts. A colourful pennant on the mainsail fluttered in a stiff, cold breeze. At the stern of the ship, on the poop deck, stood a group of officers who roared instructions as a young drummer boy beat his drum rhythmically. The ship, with three gun-decks armed with angry cannons, seemed to be swaying to the beat of the drum.

The ship was alive with feverish of activity. Marines stood to attention while the warrant officers on the quarter-deck issued instructions. Sailors waited below the masts in anticipation of orders from their petty officers. The captain turned his cheek to the wind and glanced at the masthead pendant. The ship tugged at the ropes restraining her. Inferior warrant officers issued instructions to a group of men loading provisions. It began to snow and the officers demanded more urgency.

The rusted chains that linked my ankles were thrust into my hand. The gaolers escorted me to the ship's captain. The admiral observed impassively.

"The Lord Chief Justice has decreed this day that this prisoner, guilty of high treason against the Queen of England, should be delivered at the first instance to the head gaoler of the Tower of London."

The officer turned and summoned his first lieutenant.

"Mr Gore, I place the prisoner in your charge."

The captain - an imposing figure, his body a mass of muscle - turned to address the gaoler.

"Rest assured, sir. Your prisoner is in safe hands. A galley upon the high seas is a prison without bars and chains. On an ocean voyage, there is no distinction between prisoners and sailors. Escape is quite impossible."

Mr Gore, a slim, dark-haired young man, approached and indicated for me to follow him. He led me aboard and down below the heaving deck. The rising wind was frigid and bitter, the waves dirty and grey from sand and seaweed dredged up from the ocean floor.

"Gentlemen," the captain ordered, his tone cold and decisive. "we will make sail within the hour. See that all the boats are secured. Then have the anchor hove short."

Hundreds of men, prompted by their officers, jumped to attention and clambered purposefully up and down the intricate rigging above the rolling deck. In an instant, they had unfurled the huge sails and, as a result, the ship strained harder against her ropes.

Below deck, Mr Gore extended his hand and introduced himself.

"My name is Lieutenant Gore. You are, I suspect, a victim of circumstance. A young maiden as pretty and demure as your good self can surely not be guilty of such a crime as treason?"

He was a handsome man with long, dark hair tied neatly in a black velvet bow. His hand was rough to the touch and stained with black tar from the ropes. He pushed his fringe from his forehead, exposing a savage diagonal scar that ran from his left ear to the corner of his mouth. When he was sixteen, he told me later, his father, an actor and an incessant card player, fell foul of professional gamblers. One summer's night after a play, he joined his father in a local tavern. It was a pleasant evening. On the way home, they strolled through Hyde Park. As they passed a monument, they were set upon by agents of the men to whom his father was indebted. Mr Gore, defending his father, ran his blade through the heart of one of the attackers, killing him instantly. The following morning, after being attended to by a back street doctor and fearful that his son would be imprisoned and hung, his father registered him on a merchant ship travelling to South America.

Above deck, there was freezing fog and threatening storm clouds. Below, it was dark and very cramped. The spiralling oil lanterns fixed to the timbers were black with oil and smoke. They threw strange shadows upon the faces of the men.

We moved down the narrow staircase, the companionway that linked the decks, towards the hold in the stern. We passed the ship's manger where oxen, goats and sheep were tethered along with scrawny chickens that scratched in the hay for seeds. Above, I could hear pigs squealing as they were winched on board.

Down we went, past the ship's infirmary and dispensary. A selection of crude-looking surgical instruments were on display. In the corner, in a neat pile, were a selection of wooden peg legs. The only light now was from the gratings or sky lights that reached upwards to the main deck. Lamps and candles were forbidden here as the gunpowder and ammunition were stored near the keel.

As we passed the carpenter's storeroom, we could see

an old man busily repairing the leg of a stool. We were now down below the waterline. Ponytailed sailors rushed past carrying barrels filled with water, beer and provisions. The traders and local women who had come aboard when the ship docked now made haste to disembark before the ship sailed. At the bottom of the companionway, the purser checked and recorded the barrels before they passed into the hold.

The ship heaved and groaned. We were leaving port. Mr Gore, his head bowed to avoid the low timber beams, guided me to a small cabin guarded by a red-coated marine. He opened the door and ushered me in, then closed and bolted the door behind him. A narrow beam of light came from under the door. Inside was a single wooden bowl and straw laid directly on wet timbers. The cabin was about five feet wide and not much higher. The stench of sweat, sour sea sickness and raw sewage mixed with bilge water was overpowering. It was suffocating and, to add to my horror, there were maggots everywhere.

After we had left the safety of the harbour and sailed into the boisterous Irish sea, Mr Gore returned to the cabin with ale, bread and cheese. Thankfully, he unlocked and removed my heavy chains before he left to go about his duties. Nausea from the motion of the ship and tiredness swept over me but, despite this, I slept soundly. When I woke, men's voices were roaring frantically and the ship was listing sideways.

"All hands on deck. All hands on deck."

I could clearly feel the galley lurch and creak as it was tossed from wave to wave. Suddenly, the ship rolled and rose up at a sharp angle. The monstrous wave on which the stricken galley was now riding hurled the ship forward and downwards at great speed. I fell heavily against the cabin partition. My head exploded in a confusion of sparks and light. The door to the cabin swung open. It was Mr Gore.

"Come, Grainne. I fear the ship is doomed."

I followed Mr Gore up onto the deck. It was night-time. The foam from the sea was icy, the snow in a blizzard. We ran forward, slipping on the wet planks on the quarter-deck. Above me the captain, roped to a weather rail, roared.

"Starboard … Hard to starboard!"

The deck surged up beneath us.

"Helm to starboard."

Mr Gore grabbed a rope and wrapped it around my waist, then attached it securely to the weather rail. Further along the deck, I saw an old man bending low into driving snow and salted wind. An enormous breaker curled over the weather rail. The force of its spray sent me sprawling face down on the deck. As I stood and turned to brace myself, I witnessed the unfortunate man sliding across the deck, his right hand outstretched to grasp the weather rail on the starboard side of the ship. He failed and crashed, with a blood curdling cry, into the foaming sea below.

Beyond the deck, I heard the roaring thunder of breakers pounded on rocks. The ship shuddered and grated. We had run aground. The stern was now reaching towards the sky. I was petrified with fear. My head ached.

I was securely strapped to the weather rail, but all around ashen faced men ran aimlessly along the slippery deck. Two sailors attached ropes around their waists, then jumped up on the weather rail and attempted to ease themselves down the side of the galley. An enormous wave rose behind them and mercilessly crashed down upon them. When the seawater cleared, they hung lifeless from the ropes.

Behind me, a seaman clung precariously to one end of a long section of safety rail. The rail had been partially torn away from the deck. As if in slow motion, a wave came across the bow and washed down along the deck towards the panic-stricken man. The sailor clung on, his arm wrapped around the mangled metal. Within seconds, he was dangling above a watery grave. Another wave close behind propelled man and metal into the wash.

The ship lurched and began to straighten. From behind, a strong arm grabbed hold of me. It was Mr Gore. He tried to speak, but his voice was birdlike in the howling winds. He had an axe in his hand. He indicated that he thought that the ship was about to split in two and he was going to chop down the mast. He set about cutting the weather shrouds and ratlines. This task proved very difficult. As he attempted to drive his foot through the ratlines, an icy wave pounded him from behind. The force tossed him to the deck. He must surely be dead, I feared. No man could withstand that force.

I turned into the wind and was blinded by an icy foam that stung my eyes. My body was numb. I felt no pain. I was in a dream. I looked back towards the mast. To my astonishment, Mr Gore was up and attacking the wooden mast with a ferocity I had never before witnessed. The sound of splintering rose above the mayhem and the mast tumbled, hopefully, towards the rocks. At the same time, the vessel rolled on its side. The mast fell and bounced upwards. It had landed on the rocks!

Mr Gore ran towards me. He untied the rope that secured me and led me towards the mast, now pointing down into the foaming darkness. I could see the rocks below being relentlessly battered by the tide.

Mr Gore attached my safety line to the mast and pointed towards the rocks. I hesitated, then crawled slowly out along the mast. It was wet and slippery. Within moments, I was beyond the point of no return. I stopped. Mr Gore was behind and forced me on. We had crawled beyond the weather rails and were now above the rocks and sea. I was mindful not to look down. At that moment, a wave washed over the galley and struck us from behind. I fell headlong into the surf.

Down and down I went through the freezing water, my body and brain numbed by cold and shock. In the heaving silence, my senses returned and I swam back to the surface. I broke the surface and searched for driftwood to cling on to. I reached out for a section of the mast. I spun it round in the water looking for a rope to hold on to. To my horror, it was not the mast but a drowned man. He was horribly bloated, his eyes staring and his face crushed. The air in my lungs expelled into the cold air. The sea was littered with floating bodies. My head ached as the lack of oxygen drove needles of pain into my forehead. The marrow in my bones froze. I fought for life. The relentless pounding of the waves drenched me. I could not catch my breath in the short intervals between the waves. I prayed that the next wave would propel me close to the rocks and not drag me out to sea.

All of a sudden, I could feel myself being hauled in short bursts from the raging sea. As I rose above the surface I saw Mr Gore, my safety line around his waist, his feet wedged in the crow's nest. He levered me out of the water and attached the rope to the mast. As he did so, a wave pitched him from the security of the cradle and hurled him into the icy deluge of water. Without a safety line, he disappeared into the foam.

The ship began to move forward on the rocks. If I did not proceed, I would surely perish, too.

At first I moved cautiously forward, then with a vengeance attacked the mast as if it was my mortal enemy. I could see the rocks, now less than twenty feet below. I crawled on, stopping only when the freezing foam washed over the mast. After a few moments, I felt something soft beneath my feet. I reached down. My hands were numbed. It was seaweed. I had made the rocks. Solid immovable rocks! Assured, I untied the rope from around my waist and edged forward. The seaweed was slippery. I felt around in the dark and cut my fingers on jagged rocks. I had only one wish and that was to survive. I blocked everything out. When there was no longer any seaweed, I knew that I was above the waterline and safe. Behind me, the proud galley groaned, split in two and slipped off the rocks.

It was bitterly cold. With the sound of drowning men screaming through the dark void below, I clambered blindly up the rocks onto a soft grass bank. It had stopped snowing, but the wind and sand cut into my back.

I walked for about an hour, loose wisps of salted wet hair blowing into my eyes. Mentally relieved and physically weak, I walked into the night. I just wanted to get away. It began to snow again. Up ahead was a crude labourer's cabin. It was empty, warm and filled with sweet-smelling hay. I rested and slept.

CHAPTER 7

"What have we got here, then? ... Get up girl ... Explain yourself before I set the dogs on you!"

It was an old man with a frightened girl, no more than two years old. She stood nervously behind him. It was early morning. The fields were silent and covered in a light layer of melting snow. The storm had abated. The man spoke in English. With him were two large, growling terriers, their coats black with dirt and snow. The man controlled them with a thick hawthorn stick. They sat obediently. He pointed the stick at my temple and repeated his question.

"My name is Grainne, sir. I was travelling to London by sea. Our galley ran aground during the storm last night and I swam ashore."

"I am an old man, but age has not rendered me stupid. The strand below is littered with corpses and debris from the stricken Queen's galley. At this moment, the people of the village are plundering the ship's cargo and dead. It is clear to see from your ankles that you were shackled, but it is equally clear that you are not of common labouring blood. I will be guided by my instincts and not my senses. We are poor Welsh hill farmers, but will offer you our limited hospitality."

I followed the old man as he carried the child astride

his narrow shoulders. We crossed a large open field to a row of four squalid stone hovels. These houses were single storey, but he led me beyond to an old peel tower made of stone with a thatched roof. The family lived above, their livestock below.

A narrow flight of stone steps led up to the front door. There was no handle, just a latch. The old man opened the door. The cottage was full of smoke. A log fire smouldered in the corner. It stung my eyes. An old woman sat in a rocking chair smoking a clay pipe. Against the far wall, piled high, were logs and dried cow dung. The floor was a mixture of stone and straw. The little girl now sat on a dirty, matted sheepskin rug. She had tangled nut-brown hair and wore a homespun bodice and skirt. She played with a hand-carved dog.

The old lady stood as we entered the room. She regarded me closely. The old man led me to the fire and handed me a long woollen cloak.

"Remove your wet clothes. The woman of the house will prepare a warm brew to strengthen your resolve."

I removed my clothes while the woman ladled a plate of hot oat porridge into a wooden bowl. As I ate, I watched her make up a milk drink with honey and nutmeg. I thought of Mr Gore and wondered what had become of him.

"Later, I will take you to Rhyl Castle," the old man said. "The Duke of Harlech will know what best to do with you. He has two young daughters and a son your age. You would make an interesting companion for them."

Later that afternoon, warmed in body and soul, I bade farewell to the woman and her daughter and followed the man on the short walk through the estate to Rhyl Castle. It was a pleasant day, but still deathly cold. We climbed a small hill. At the summit, a stark, lonely castle appeared. The proud, rough, stone ancestral home of the Duke of

Harlech had splendid panoramic views of the coastline from Llandudno to Prestatyn.

We followed the ramparts to the moat and crossed over the drawbridge. The castle steward reluctantly led us to the Duke of Harlech's private rooms. We followed him up the stone staircase four floors to the top of the castle. The building was dank, cold and gloomy. We passed the narrow slit windows behind which many bowmen had plied their trade for centuries. It was surprising how much light came through these narrow windows. In the Duke's private apartments, we found Lord and Lady Harlech and their family. While the ground floor of the castle was of earth and the following floors of wood, this floor was stone flagged. The room was surprisingly well furnished with expensive rugs and tapestries. While the furniture in Ballinacor House was basic and functional, here it was ornate and delicately gilded in gold leaf.

"My Lord, excuse our intrusion. I deliver to you a pitiful young woman. I believe her to be the sole survivor of the shipwreck at Hunter's Cove. She is of ..."

There was a commotion outside. A drumbeat came from the fields below and echoed around the castle walls. The Duke of Harlech peered through a slit window, then ran to the battlements Fires were being lit and there was the clear outline of colourful tents being erected in the snow. He returned and spoke to the steward.

"Steward, the time has come. The Crown soldiers will not be repelled. They have arrived in force and are camped strategically, encircling the castle. Escape is impossible. We must pay now for the warring deeds of our ancestors. Is it not enough that they have confiscated our lands and murdered my father and brother? If I offer myself as a hostage, our followers and Lady Harlech will be spared and the girls placed in the Queen's service.

"In order that the family line should continue, Richard, my only son, must escape. While I go above and divert the Crown's attention, take Richard and our guest below to the tunnel. Provide them with sufficient food and clothing to carry them to London."

The steward bowed his head and watched impassively as Richard briefly embraced his family. These were hard times with little time for sentiment.

"Richard," the Duke of Harlech said as he walked to a gilt writing desk. "You must travel directly to London, to the home of your uncle, William Wycherley. Deliver this letter and remain there until otherwise instructed."

We ran down the stairs, following the steward. Richard was a strong, athletic young man, tall and handsome with long chestnut hair tied back. He wore a simple snuff-brown suit with a white ruffled shirt. His dark brown riding boots clicked on the stone steps as we descended.

When we reached the ground level, the steward went down on his knees and, with his bare hands, began dragging at the loose red clay. After awhile, a wooden trapdoor appeared below the raised dust. An oil lamp was lowered into the eerie darkness.

Richard jumped down into the tunnel. There was a squeal as rats scampered in all directions. I followed. The steward bade us good fortune, then closed the trapdoor above. Richard held the lamp above his head and led me away from the castle. I became concerned as the damp clay walls appeared to close in on me. As we walked, small pieces of earth fell from the roof. Seawater began to seep up from below.

The walls now became sandy and less stable. Richard, to my annoyance, found my anxiety humorous. Soon the tunnel narrowed and the roof height dropped. We had to crawl on our hands and knees. The seawater was rising rapidly.

For a moment, I stopped and began to panic. I tried to turn back. Richard crawled out of view. I scrambled forward, the roof of the tunnel crumbling behind me. A section fell and trapped my legs. Frantically, I dug my nails deep into the damp sand ahead of me and pulled with all my might. Kicking and dragging in the dark, I eventually managed to free myself. In a frenzy, I crawled blindly, feeling my way further down the tunnel. To my relief, I could hear the tide lapping on the shore and see narrow beams of daylight.

As we emerged onto the beach, Richard held up his hand and pointed to the rock face above. Soldiers, their cloaks tossed by the wind, stood guarding the shore.

The beach was deserted and stretched for miles. We moved swiftly over the shingle until we came to a small cottage. Here we moved inland until we reached a remote two-storey farmhouse. Richard ran around the back. Minutes later, he returned leading two fine dark bay horses.

"I presume, Grainne, that you can ride?" Richard asked sarcastically.

"But of course, sir," I replied, vaulting up on the horse's back.

We galloped along the coastal paths until we reached Prestatyn. Here, we rested, fed and watered the horses. Daylight was fading. Richard brought me to a tavern and ordered a bottle of claret and venison pie. In the corner, a drunken man was preaching.

"Yes, gentlemen. I may be a Mathematician, but that does not render me unqualified to have opinions on other matters. I stand by my statement. Despise as you will the Frenchman, once England and France were part of the same continent."

Richard, now warmed by the fine French wine, interjected rudely, "Sir, as a matter of debate, I am of the opinion that we do not fully understand scripture as a tangible and current subject. Yet you speak about the primeval formation of the continents. Your argument, sir, I suggest is shrouded in presumption."

From the corner of the tavern, a clergyman moved forward from the shadows and regarded us angrily.

"De gustibus non est disputandum," he roared across the room. His attention was diverted by two dogs who snarled and fought over an ox bone.

"Sir, I consider," he continued, grinding his teeth, "that your comments are born from ignorance. And since you have, it appears, not been taught Latin by the Queen's tutors, you are insufficiently educated to have an opinion."

Richard, his spirit aggrieved, continued.

"The Pope, sir," Richard continued, "has found the Queen of England guilty of heresy against the Catholic Church. He claims rightly that Catholics are responsible only to St Peter and the Church in Rome. The Queen and her church have no jurisdiction over Christians!"

The mood in the tavern became perilous. Everyone turned to inspect the young agitator. The landlord wisely interjected and, without further consideration, expelled Richard forcibly from the tavern.

We collected the horses, remounted and followed the road signs for Chester. It was still cold, but the night was clear. By the time we reached the outskirts of Chester, the snow had almost disappeared. We were moving south.

We stopped at a crossroads. Richard pointed to a fire burning in a field close by. It was a gypsy encampment. Their horses grazed along the hedgerows. In the field, the painted gypsy caravans circled a campfire. Up to fifty Romany men, women and children were singing and dancing to the accompaniment of fiddles and bagpipes. They paid little attention to us as we approached.

We dismounted. Richard spoke to an elderly woman seated upon a three-legged stool. Her face was visibly scarred by the harshness of her life. Her brass earrings reflected the warm fire at our backs. Richard offered her six pence to read his fortune. The woman placed the money between what was left of her rotten teeth, then dropped the coin into the bodice of her mud-splattered dress. She took Richard's hand and ran a long, dirty, cracked nail along his life-line. In shock, she dropped his hand, stood up and walked away.

"Tell me, woman. What do you see?" Richard shouted as he ran after her.

"Young master, you surely do not wish this fine young woman to bear witness to your misfortune."

"I have no fears. I command you to inform me of my fate."

She looked at Richard with pity and fear, then relented.

"I see before me a withered flower, a rope and many women crying. Your family has been cursed. Young master, life and love will not flow through your veins."

I moved to the campfire. That night, I slept under a blanket by the blazing fire listening to the haunting strains of an old gypsy woman singing laments.

I woke at dawn. Richard, despondent, sat beside me. In the distance, a red gypsy caravan approached. As it came closer, I could see a young, dark-haired woman seated beside an enormous bearded man, his shirt open to the waist defying the elements. He was a man of fifty years or more. He stood almost seven foot tall and had muscles that rippled and threatened to burst from his clothing. His brown, parchment-like face was stained from the smoke of a thousand campfires. Behind him, mischievous young children sang as the caravan swayed, its pots and pans rattling and crashing against the tailboard.

"The King of the Gypsies," Richard said pointing to the man. "He has been informed that there is a young pretender to his crown camped here. He has travelled this day to quell the rising and reinforce his standing."

The King of the Gypsies dismounted from the caravan and called out to those who dared to challenge his supremacy.

"I am told that there is a young man in this camp foolish enough to challenge the King of the Gypsies. If that be so, let him present himself!"

The gypsies parted to allow their champion to come forward. The King of the Gypsies regarded the young man with disdain and retorted in a mocking laugh.

"Have I travelled all this way, ha ha ha, to battle with a young man as yet unable to grow a beard? I will not fight or wrestle this feeble young warrior. I have no wish to kill him or any man. I will, however, confirm my advantage by challenging him to a contest of skill and strength."

"You are indeed King of the Gypsies," the challenger roared confidently, "and at liberty to choose by what means you relinquish your title. I accept your challenge on your terms."

The King of the Gypsies picked up a lead rope and walked over to where the horses were grazing. Selecting a grey cob, he attached the rein to its halter and called for his eldest son to lead the horse twenty paces away. He removed his laced boots and called to the gypsies to stand back. In his bare feet he ran at the horse. One stride from the startled animal, he sprang from his right leg, threw forward his left and easily cleared the animal's withers without disturbing a single hair on its back. The King of the Gypsies turned triumphantly and saluted the assembled, but silent, crowd.

He then walked towards the confused animal and calmed her by stroking her long white mane. The horse stood quite still. With his right hand holding onto the velvet of her muzzle, he unexpectedly drew himself back, crouched, dropped his right hand and grasped the horse round the knees. At the same instant, his left arm spread around her hocks. Before the horse knew what was happening, he had lifted her clean off the ground. He bore the weight of the horse on his broad shoulders as a hunter might carry a dead deer. Bent almost double, he moved forward one step, two step, three, four, five … The horse's hind legs strained against the King of the Gypsies arms. Six steps … The horse kicked out with one of her forefeet. He stumbled forward. Seven, eight … His lungs were now about to burst. His head began to spin. Nine steps … Ten. He fell forward. The horse's hoof caught him on the side of the head. The King of the Gypsies fell to the ground. The horse galloped off.

When he stood, the challenger had withdrawn. The King of the Gypsies ordered the children back into the caravan. Within minutes, he had left the campsite and was heading for Liverpool.

We breakfasted on red herrings, oat cakes and broth and left the campsite within the hour. The weather had picked up considerably and the sun began to shine.

Richard abandoned the road to Worcester and we headed off across the fields. We rode through wild, overgrown valleys, along narrow paths bordered by alders and willow trees, down past a brown, fast-moving river and up again through a copse of beech trees. As we reached the brow of a hill, a herd of fallow deer scattered in all directions. They pranced across the wide open vista that opened up before our eyes. Richard spurred his horse on. The horse laid back its ears and propelled itself forward into a gallop. Rejoicing in their freedom, the horses crossed the fields in seconds.

We rode all day, stopping only on the outskirts of

Wellington to rest and change the horses. We arrived in Worcester exhausted and saddle sore. It was ten o'clock in the evening. It was cold and very dark. Richard's aunt lived in Worcester and we made our way towards her grand manor house.

Aunt Mary greeted us coldly, but graciously. She brought us directly to the kitchens, where the cook served up a grand meal: oysters to start, followed by stewed carp, pork and boiled beef. Fed and warmed, we were brought to our rooms by the housekeeper. A maidservant was lighting the fire in my chamber as I entered. A change of clothes had been provided and lay on the ornate four-poster bed. Another maidservant came out of an adjoining room.

"Your hot tub is drawn, miss."

I bathed and dressed in a plum-coloured silk dress with contrasting pale blue petticoats. I laughed when Richard called to escort me to the drawing room. He looked quite ridiculous in a pink satin suit with black stockings and square-toed shoes covered in velvet with a matching bow in his hair.

As we entered the drawing room, we interrupted an elderly woman whose features were obscured beneath a hideous blonde wig. She turned and extended a freckled hand that was beautifully manicured but knotted and twisted by rheumatism.

"Catholics," she continued, "are wicked men who worship heathen statues and take orders from a scarlet monster who lives in Rome."

She spoke to a tall elegant woman with cascading chestnut-coloured hair framing rich ruby lips. Her complexion was pale. She wore no jewellery or make-up, just a simple garnet brooch which gathered her elegant taffeta dress below the bustle.

For the first time since I had met Richard, we spoke at

length. I was, of course, evasive, but he was expansive in relating his family fortunes. His father, despite his pleasant public persona, was a drunken tyrant whose death few would mourn. He spent most of his time in London with a string of young mistresses. His time in Rhyl with his family was solely limited to collecting rents and fulfilling his duties as lord.

We sat by the fire and spoke for hours. Richard was an innocent young man, a victim of the turbulent times he lived in. He had never known love. But yet, despite his circumstances, he maintained and percolated a wealth of affection and a sense of fun.

When he was sixteen, he rode to Llandudno on an errand for his father. While clearing a ditch, his horse fell and broke its leg. Richard ran to a local cottage in search of a man with a gun so that he could put the unfortunate animal out of its misery. At the house, he met a slim young girl he described as the most beautiful creature he had ever set eyes upon.

"Her eyes exuded youthful laughter, excitement and devilment. Her fiery red hair fell like tossed flames on her shoulders. She had a gentle disposition and her complexion was as soft and translucent as the finest porcelain."

Richard fell perilously in love with Eleanor. Each Sunday thereafter they met secretly in the local church. Over the following months, their youthful affection turned to a lavish, deep-seated love.

One cold and wet Sunday evening, however, as Richard sheltered from the driving rain in the church, his simple world was thrown into disarray. He found an envelope at the base of the iron waterfont. Inside was a letter and a small spray of dried autumnal flowers. Brittle leaves fell from the envelope and scattered on the stone entrance porch.

*Farewell, sir. I will never forget you. It is better that we
never meet again. I cannot live in your world nor you in mine.
I will love you always.*
Eleanor

Richard immediately abandoned the secrecy of their relationship and rode stubbornly to Eleanor's cottage. To his dismay, her mother informed him that she had left home that morning.

When the story of his relationship was related back to the Duke of Harlech, Richard was immediately dispatched to London to the home of his Uncle William in order that he might select a more suitable partner.

The mantle clock struck twelve. Exhausted, I excused myself and went to bed.

The following morning, with a packed lunch, clean clothes and full stomachs, we set out on the final leg of our journey to London.

As we passed through Banbury in the early afternoon, we came across a local festival. It was a cold, but clear, day. Young village girls with wreaths of seasonal wild flowers in their hair tossed leaves from their aprons onto the roadway. On a street corner, the blacksmith played the fiddle while, further along the crowded street, two men dressed in kilts played the bagpipes. Before them men, women and children danced jigs.

In the square, there was a team of hardy wrestlers on a raised platform. Men placed wagers on the possible outcome. A group of women were passing a hot, loving cup called Sack-Posset, a drink made from hot milk, wine and spices. The chaplain, an aspiring magician, entertained a group of children while nurses and maids from the big houses held on to the hands of their young charges. We changed our horses once again and headed on for Aylesbury.

The road to London from Chester had been almost deserted, save for the odd farmer moving his cattle or haggard woman carrying great bundles of brushwood. Now it widened and became congested with horses and carriages. There were scores of people hacking and hiking to the capital in search of commerce and employment. We crossed stone bridges and galloped up muddy roads bending low across our horses' withers to avoid stout, overhanging limbs of beech trees. It was a wild, lawless and fascinating time.

When we reached Whitchurch, it was already dark. It began to rain and we entered a tavern in search of food and lodgings. The Cock and Hen was a miserable, dark, dusty tavern crowded with men and women standing and sitting at small crude wooden tables. Everybody clutched tankards of frothing ale and picked from dishes of fresh whitebait. Richard ordered ale and roasted fowl pullets. We sat before the open fire. A group of men behind us played cards.

All of a sudden, the door to the tavern burst open. A cold, icy wind blew through the tavern, tossing the flames in the fireplace. A loud, harsh voice bellowed.

"Richard, son of the Duke of Harlech, I arrest you in the name of Queen Elizabeth. You are to be delivered this night to the Tower of London and detained at Her Majesty's pleasure."

Richard and I turned. In shock, I watched as he was taken from the tavern and dragged out into the night. All that remained was his unfinished tankard of ale, two shillings and the letter his father, the Duke of Harlech, gave him to deliver to his uncle, William Wycherley, in London.

CHAPTER 8

I wandered around Whitchurch for hours hoping that Richard would somehow re-appear. At midnight, despondent, I returned to the blacksmith and hired a horse. Minutes later, I walked aimlessly from the security of the village to follow the road to London.

As dawn spread across the horizon, London appeared with its smoking chimneys and myriad of church spires, their bells pealing as if to announce my arrival. I rode through Edgeware, Islington, and Bethnal Green. The raised pavements heralded my return to civilisation.

I was not prepared for the hustle and bustle of London - the narrow, cobbled streets and alleys, the poverty and wealth, the colour and pageantry and, most of all, the noise level. London was the centre of administration and power of the empire. It was a bustling, noisy city that exhumed a pervasive, variable stench from sewerage, rotting vegetables and coal smoke. The clamour never ceased - the rumbling of drays on the cobbles, the clatter of horse hooves and the incessant cries from street vendors.

"Apples, oranges, cockles and oysters!"

Ahead was a street sign: Spitalfields. The name sounded vaguely familiar ... I remembered. This was where Dr. McKinnon's mother ran the Royal Oak tavern. I decided to try to seek lodgings there.

Spitalfields was the centre of London's silk industry. The narrow streets were lined with small weavers' cottages. Hanging from the whitewashed walls of many of these simple artisan homes were cages of thrushes and linnets.

At the Royal Oak, Mrs McKinnon answered the door. She was a small, demure woman with a broad cockney accent. She looked with obvious scorn at the travel-stained girl who had arrived unannounced on her doorstep.

"My name is Grainne," I explained. "I am a friend of James's. I am alone and in need of lodgings!"

"I am not a wealthy woman," she replied, "but I am curious of James's progress and I do have a pressing need for a serving wench. I can offer you a shilling a week along with your board and lodgings."

That night, I tended the tables. The drowsy heat inside the tavern enfolded me like a warm blanket. It was a shocking, moving experience. The dregs of society, it seemed, had congregated in the Royal Oak. It was the definitive den of iniquity loaded with a vast and formidable array of characters - men who studied the faces of their playing cards and opponents and women who studied the men.

"Drunk for 1d, Dead drunk 2d," claimed the sign over the bar. Apart from ale and wine, there were numerous other drinks: Metheglin, a sweet honey drink, Mum, an ale made from wheat, Tanzy eggs, a drink made from cream and dry white Spanish wine, and Hypocras, a mixture of wines and spices.

The following day was Sunday. Mrs McKinnon invited me to join her on a riverboat trip to St James's Park. We took a carriage to the Tower Pier. Mrs McKinnon pointed out the imposing and fortified Tower of London.

Mindful that Richard was incarcerated somewhere in

this foreboding Tower, I confided in Mrs McKinnon and informed her of the Duke of Harlech's letter. Mrs McKinnon said she would arrange a carriage to take me to William Wycherley's house that night.

A failing wind and a falling tide carried us towards Westminster Pier. As we approached London Bridge, there were hundreds of sailors, children, gypsies and dock workers fishing for whitebait. The incoming tide pushed the whitebait by their millions against the wall of the Naval Hospital. Baskets were being lowered into the brown waters of the Thames alive with the flurry of these tiny fish. These insignificant fish were Greenwich's most important industry. Each successful fisherman had a blanket or tub of wriggling glittering minnows.

London Bridge now towered above us. The oily, misty, sewage-infested river was alive with endless traffic. Ships flying flags from Sweden, Turkey and Portugal were piloted up the river carrying figs, indigo and spices from the far side of the world. Barges and galleys were unloading drunken pleasure-seekers at Westminster Pier.

As we pulled in, a riverman reached out for the bow of our boat and drew her to the bottom step. Against the wall of the pier was a naked man, floating face down in the Thames. A curious child poked at the corpse with a stick. The body rolled over in the water. Mrs McKinnon turned away.

"The body was here last Sunday. It is an unfortunate Negro slave," Mrs McKinnon said.

The body of the Negro, I observed, had turned a strange, white, marble colour in the water.

We hurried through the crowded lanes to James's Park, skipping past the endless flocks of ragged beggars. In the park, we strolled beneath an avenue of elm and lime trees, fed the tame roe deer and drank wine in a tavern close to

Queen Anne's Gate. As we left the tavern, a band of performing Romanies appeared leading a scrawny brown bear on a heavy linked chain. I could see that his paws were bleeding and that the chain was cutting into old sores on his neck. The bear's handler began poking the unfortunate animal, instructing him to rise on his hind legs for our benefit. The bear growled and lunged forward at his tormentor. Behind him, another Romany had a ragged monkey on his shoulder. He, too, was attached to a link chain. The second Romany, observing our disdain at the condition and treatment of the bear, removed the monkey from his shoulder and swung it to and fro by its tail. The monkey squealed in pain. The two Romany men laughed in unison and ran off down the street.

Judging by their lack of interest, Londoners were well accustomed to such barbarity.

It was almost dark when we returned to the Royal Oak for supper. Later, as promised, Mrs McKinnon arranged for a carriage to carry me to Finsbury Square in order to deliver the letter to Richard's uncle, William Wycherley.

"A noted playwright and womaniser," warned Mrs McKinnon.

The carriage stopped in the cobbled square. Children ran races around the park. The houses were modest, but comfortable. I climbed the six granite steps to the front door. I pulled the bell. It rang loudly inside. A manservant opened the door.

"The Wycherley residence."

I explained that I had a letter for the master from the Duke of Harlech. He left me standing on the step and rudely closed the door in my face. Minutes later, a middle-aged man wearing a brocaded dressing gown opened the door.

"Thank God," he declared, grasping the letter. "But

where is young Richard? Is he not with you? I received distressing reports this morning that Lord and Lady Harlech have been put to death by the Queen's army and that Richard and a young female companion had escaped."

He began to read the letter.

"Excuse my manners. I am William Wycherley, a humble playwright. Please join me in my drawing room."

Mr Wycherley listened intently to my story.

"Tomorrow at first light we will take a carriage to the Tower. In the interim, I will make the necessary arrangements with the Governor. You will stay here as my guest. I will send word to Mrs McKinnon."

The following morning at eight o'clock, Mr Wycherley and I approached the Tower of London. The entrance to the Tower was beneath an iron portcullis guarded by grim looking sentries. We presented our passes and were led across the drawbridge.

At the Byward Tower, we had to give the daily password. Today it was "The Archbishop." We were now admitted to the great turreted stone castle. After passing through the original castle, we were led on to Tower Green and then, finally, to the Beauchamp Tower, where Richard was imprisoned.

An indifferent gaoler unlocked the door and indicated for us to follow the winding stone stairs upwards. The stench was foul. I placed my handkerchief over my mouth and nose. The turnkey at the top of the stairs unlocked the door to the cell without uttering a word.

The solitary window in the cell was barred and buried deep in grey stone walls which were three feet thick. A single candle flickered over the damp walls. On the stone floor was straw for a bed and a bucket for a toilet. Richard lay in the corner face down on the straw. He sobbed despairingly. Outside, there was a flourish of trumpets from

Tower Hill. A gilded coach drawn by six grey horses passed. Beefeaters marched proudly on each side of the coach.

Richard turned to see who had entered the cell. His leg irons grated on the stone floor. He held a wooden crucifix in his hand.

"Grainne, Uncle William, I am so glad to see you. I did not expect you. You must fetch me a priest. I cannot die with so many sins on my soul."

A bolt shot, a key turned and the door swung back on heavy hinges. The gaoler entered the cell and spoke to William.

"Sir, it is plain to see that the young prisoner is both penniless and despondent and as such suffers, as common men, the worst horrors of the Tower. I can also see that you are a man of substance. Surely your wish should be that your young friend's last hours be made as comfortable as possible."

"What are you saying, man?" William asked impatiently.

"Sir, you are obviously not versed in the workings of the Tower of London. I am Lord of these hallowed walls and all incarcerated within. For a small remuneration, however, I can offer the condemned man religious solace, congenial accommodation and a supply of fine Jamaican rum. Rum, sir, numbs the brain, cures all ills and inspires the inner strength necessary to face the executioner."

"You are an insolent man," retorted William. "You, of course, leave me no alternative."

William handed the gaoler a purse. The man studied the contents. Richard stood, gathered his composure, and paced the cell.

"What news is there of my father and mother?" he enquired. William replied solemnly.

"The reports, I'm afraid, are not favourable. They say

that your sisters have been sent to Scotland, placed in the Queen's service ... The news, however, of Lord and Lady Harlech is ... not so congenial ... We have been advised that they were put to death."

Richard turned and faced the wall. He placed both hands on its damp stone surface and allowed his head to fall between his shoulders. He was destitute.

The door of the cell opened. A young priest entered. He was a tall, slender man with a dark beard trimmed to a point. Richard, resigned to his fate, fell to his knees and beseeched the priest to absolve him of his sins and prepare him for the next world.

"Your God has forsaken me, sir! The gypsy woman predicted it. I beseech you to prepare my soul for the next world!"

William and I left Richard with the only man capable of consoling him.

William escorted me to the carriage and ordered the coachman to convey me to Finsbury Square. He returned later that afternoon, remorseful. He had exerted as much pressure and influence as he could on his peers, without success. Richard was to be executed the following morning.

I went to my room and tried to read. It was impossible I could not concentrate. All I could see was Richard's barren face.

A maidservant knocked and entered my room. She laid a black taffeta dress on the bed and informed me that Mr Wycherley's play was being premièred that night and I should dress appropriately.

Later, I joined William in the library. He was nervous. He had invited the Duchess of Kent, an avid supporter of the theatre in London, to be his guest at the opening. Her arrival was imminent.

The doorbell rang. In the hall, the manservant shuffled

to the door. William stiffened and nervously turned to face his guests.

The Duchess swept into the room with the self-assurance brought about by wealth, power and unquestioned beauty. She was resplendent in a flowing red velvet dress emblazoned with a vulgar display of remarkable jewels. This woman was well capable of corrupting the body and soul of any man she chose. She settled on a navy blue chaise lounge and gracefully arranged her skirts. Completed to her satisfaction, she folded the ruffles of her sleeves then flicked open her oriental gauze fan and lowered her long, dark eyelashes. She drank a glass of claret.

Outside in the square, beggars marvelled at the magnificent coach in which the Duchess had just arrived. Many of them even climbed the trees hoping to catch a glimpse of the notorious Duchess and her latest beau, Gregory, who sat silently and obediently beside her. The wall lamp highlighted his youthful freckles, poorly concealed by heavy powder. His sea-blue eyes were full of zest, sparkle and mischief. He was dressed in a scarlet coat with gold braid and carried a general's hat tufted with cock feathers.

Gregory sat opposite me in the gilded coach. He could have been no more than sixteen years old. He pulled the coach window down and inhaled the cold wintry air. The Duchess instructed him to close it immediately. Gregory bowed his head in a gesture of hurt. The Duchess responded by running a gloved finger across his cheek. Gregory, reassured, raised his head and smiled.

We reclined on blue satin cushions as the coach rumbled along on the uneven cobblestones. Six proud grey horses, their tails braided in colourful ribbons, pulled the coach. The postillion sat upon one of the leading horses, demanding that the pedestrians and traffic make way for the Duchess's coach. William, who had been euphoric leaving Finsbury Square, now sat in silence, staring passively out the window of the coach. The Duchess allowed him his contemplative time.

At the Theatre Royal we were greeted with a fanfare of trumpets, fireworks and a plush red carpet. While the Duchess and William were being introduced to the actors, I read the promotional poster:

THE COUNTRY WIFE
A romantic comedy by
William Wycherley
Vice, Virtue, Love and Honour
Starring
George Gore and Elizabeth Wheetley
Nightly at 8. p.m.
Matinee Saturday and Sunday at 3.p.m.

George Gore ... Could this be Mr Gore's father? I looked at the tall, slender, aristocratic man in earnest conversation with the Duchess. The resemblance was apparent.

The introductions and pleasantries completed, we were escorted to the royal box in the centre of the theatre. Below us was an astounding array of people, considerably more animated and interesting than the actors. Whores, aristocrats and professional men fervently contributed to the utter mayhem inside the theatre. The subdued, eloquent and honourable citizens of London mixed freely with the spurious, who meandered through the dark and narrow aisles in a haze of musk.

The curtain rose. The play began. The orchestra, situated under the stage, were barely audible The crowd became silent. The play was a comedy with an implausible plot. The hero, the man I presumed to be Mr Gore's father, was a handsome, witty, urban aristocrat who had fallen on hard times. He had come to the city in search of fame and fortune.

The audience soon tired and became restless. A group of men in the pit began cat-calling. A drunken woman, drowned in gin and rum, leaned back and tossed a ripe tomato on the stage. The theatre, in unison, erupted with people standing and hurling abuse at the startled actors.

William and the Duchess exited. Gregory and I followed close behind.

CHAPTER 9

I tossed and turned all night. All I could see was Richard's young bewildered face lined with tears.

"Fetch me a priest. I cannot die with so many sins on my soul."

The Judge appears, smiling broadly as he passes sentence on Richard, "It is incumbent upon me to sentence you to death. The unanimous verdict of the jury is that you are guilty as charged. You will be returned this day to the Tower of London. On Tuesday next, at dawn, you will be taken from the Tower to the place of execution where you will be hanged by the neck until you are dead. May God have mercy on your soul."

"Fetch me a priest. I cannot die with so many sins on my soul."

Below, the grandfather clock in the hall chimed the hours. One o'clock, two, three, four, five. At six, I dressed and moved downstairs. The reception rooms that had been alive with drunken revellers a few hours earlier were now deserted and silent. William slept, breathing rhythmically in a winged fireside chair. I shook him gently.

"It is close to daylight," I whispered.

A bottle of brandy fell to the floor.

"Richard is due to be hanged this morning," I added.

William opened his bleary eyes and grunted.

"The child's soul is saved. He has his priest. What more can I do? I have my own problems. Leave me alone, girl. Disturb me once again and I will have you thrown out onto the streets!"

I grabbed my cloak and ran out the front door. Fortunately, a coachman was resting against the park railings. I asked him to carry me to the Tower.

I arrived as daylight was breaking. The Middlesex sheriffs had just arrived at the gates. They demanded of the Lieutenant Governor that Richard the Lord of Harlech be delivered to them for execution.

I called out to Richard as he was placed in the black mourning coach drawn by four dark bay horses. The priest and two warders walked ceremoniously alongside the coach escorted by twenty foot guards, their bayonets fixed. A drummer boy beat his drum. The mood was solemn. A small curious crowd gathered and followed the horse guards on the march to Whitehall.

An unruly, impatient crowd waited in Whitehall. People had been queuing all night for the best vantage points. A public hanging was a social event.

A large wooden structure had been erected against the imposing stone walls of a church. The sides of the platform were draped in black serge. Richard emerged from the mourning coach and followed the priest into a small booth built at the base of the scaffolding. Here Richard was given the last rights.

A company of horse guards armed with pikes stood three deep circling the perimeter of the platform. Above stood four other men - the priest, two public officials, one of which read the declaration, and the executioner.

The crowd had become agitated and restless. Richard, dressed in a white ruffled shirt, removed his flaxen wig and bowed honourably to the officials as he fingered the wooden crucifix that hung around his neck. For a moment, Richard considered the angry, baying crowd gathering before him. The priest approached reading aloud from his Bible. Richard fell to his knees and blessed himself. The priest lay the Bible on his head.

The public official read out the charges and judgement levelled at Richard. The hangman checked the trapdoor mechanism. Twice it failed to open.

Richard, oblivious, stood before the rope as it swung in a gentle but chilling breeze. The executioner rolled down the collar of Richard's ruffled shirt and placed the noose roughly around his neck. Richard handed the executioner a sum of money. The hood was placed over his head. He stood awhile, then raised his hand to signal his readiness. His coffin stood open beneath the scaffold.

The executioner moved across the platform to the trapdoor. After a short deliberation, he pulled the lever. The crowd surged forward. Richard's body fell through the void. The rope immediately became taught. For a moment, Richard's athletic body jerked upwards, trying to fight the rope strangling him. Slowly, his body stiffened and he went limp. The rope now swung to and fro like a pendulum.

A woman in front turned quickly and brushed against me. I remembered Richard's description:

"Her fiery red hair fell like tossed flames on her shoulders. Her complexion was as soft and translucent as the finest porcelain."

Tears flowed down the woman's rose-coloured cheeks. In one hand she held a sprig of dried flowers, in the other a handsome young boy.

Eleanor?

I felt as limp-jointed as a puppet and fell backwards. A man caught me as I fell. I turned … It was Mr Gore.

CHAPTER 10

Mr. Gore led me through the dispersing crowd to a small teahouse. I was bemused but delighted that the man who had so willingly tendered his life for mine was alive. Inexplicably, I cried. Mr. Gore put a comforting arm around my shoulders. I noticed two fingers of his left hand were missing. He led me to a quiet corner and ordered sweet milk and cheesecake. He was curious as to why I should be attending the hanging of a man guilty of high treason. I explained. In return, he relived his horrific ordeal in the freezing waters off the coast of Rhyl.

"I plunged headlong into the foaming sea. As I reached the surface, a huge wave rolled in and carried me, fortuitously, onto jagged rocks festooned with the bloated bodies of dead sailors. By morning, I was frozen solid and riddled with frostbite"

Mr. Gore held up his ravaged hand with the missing fingers, "but I was gratified that fate had granted me the opportunity to turn this terrible tragedy to my advantage. The authorities would, in due course, be notified that Mr. Gore, wanted for murder, is presumed dead, lost at sea."

"How did you get to London?" I enquired.

"I stole a horse and rode to Liverpool. At the port, I was told that one of the O'Malley galleys from the west of

Ireland had put in for provisions. I appealed to Granuaile, the leader of her clan and a legendary sea captain. As I had sailed as an officer with Sir Francis Drake and am well-versed in navigating the murky and congested River Thames, she succumbed and offered me free passage to London."

"Why did she sail here to London. Surely she is regarded as an enemy of the Queen of England?"

"She has little option. The Crown has confiscated her lands in Connaught and murdered her son Owen. Tibbot, another son, is being held hostage by an agent of the Queen and Donal, her brother, has been gaoled. Granuaile, vigilant to safeguard her estates and re-establish her existence, has pleaded a voluntary submission to the Queen of England. She wrote and appealed to the Crown and has subsequently been granted an audience. She is staying in London at the moment in home of Thomas, Duke of Ormond."

A woman with fiery red hair and pale skin the texture of cream had been shamelessly listening to our conversation. She stood and offered Mr. Gore her hand.

"I beg your pardon, sir," she whispered. Her hand appeared to be crafted from fine bone china, her fingers long and slender. She had a charm, beauty and natural ability to capture Mr. Gore's undivided attention.

"Pray, sir, tell me about the infamous Sir Francis Drake! You have sailed with this man? Is he an honest seafarer and adventurer or a common pirate?"

"Madame, that is for you to decide. I can report that I sailed on the flagship the Golden Hind from Plymouth harbour with Sir Francis. We were in a fleet of five ships that set sail for South America. For sixteen days, the galleys were assaulted by wind and sea. The only ship to survive was the Golden Hind. Alone on the vast Pacific Ocean, we gave chase to a solitary Spanish galleon bound for Panama. On the equator, the hunter snared his prey. In minutes, we boarded and disabled the galleon. It took four days, however, to plunder her monstrous booty of gold, silver, pearls and precious stones. The hunter now became the hunted. To avoid the might of the pursuing Spanish fleet, we set sail for England round North America by way of the Arctic Ocean.

"Howling gales drove us back. We returned to Plymouth by way of the Indian Ocean and the Cape of Good Hope. Queen Elizabeth, delighted with the return on her investment, knighted the first Englishman to circumnavigate the world. The King of Spain ordered that an armada of sixty craft be primed to exact retribution. Sir Francis, with a small mobile fleet and mindful that attack in this instance was the best form of defence, set sail for Cadiz and destroyed the armada as it lay in the harbour.

"'That will singe the beard of the King of Spain,' laughed Sir Francis as we sailed triumphantly from Cadiz harbour.

"The Spanish rebuilt and doubled the size of their armada and set out for England, sailing in a crescent formation eight miles wide. We put to sea with orders not to attack the main formation, but to cut out and isolate the Spanish galleons one by one. For ten days we sailed rings around the armada. In disarray, the Spanish fled through the Straits of Dover bound for the North Sea. A deep, angry depression spread across the northern sky. Sir Francis, weather-wise, ran the fleet to harbour at the Firth of Forth.

"North around Scotland swept the armada, past the dangerous reefs of Skye, hurled and abused by the force of a fearsome gale sent by Satan. On they ran to the thunderous west coast of Ireland, where many despondent sailors, soldiers and priests filled their belts and pockets with gold and silver and dived into the raging sea. From the surf they staggered to be met by the Irish, who gratefully relieved them of their riches.

"Sir Francis, madame, I am proud to advise, saved England from the Spanish Armada without losing a single ship."

Mr. Gore and I bade the woman farewell and took a brisk stroll through St. James's Park. It was now wet and misty. Mr. Gore confessed that our meeting in Whitehall was not an accident. He saw me the previous night at the première standing outside the Theatre Royal. When he realised that I was in the company of the Duchess, he was confused and convinced that I would not welcome his interruption. However, he followed me to the Wycherley residence and from there to Whitehall this morning.

We walked and talked all day until dusk ushered in a cold chill.

"Shall I escort you back to Finsbury Square?" Mr. Gore enquired.

In the excitement and confusion, I had not considered that my tenuous links with William Wycherley were now severed. I had to find a safe passage back to Ireland. Grace O'Malley, the woman known as Granuaile the Pirate Queen, came from Connaught. Surely, I thought, when her audience with the Queen is concluded she will return to Connaught. I was not cheered by the prospect of sailing, but there was no alternative.

"Mr. Gore," I queried. "Do you think that Granuaile would allow me to travel back to Ireland with her?"

"I cannot think, Grainne, why you should wish to leave London and return to such a barbaric, lawless country. But there is much about you that I could never hope to understand. I will take you directly to the home of Thomas, Duke of Ormond, where Granuaile and her cohorts are residing."

The house, in a small square off Regent Street, was one of a row of commodious new homes built of red brick and stone. It was dark now. Mr. Gore and I climbed the steps to the entrance porch. Inside the bay-windowed house, I could see refined men and women in feverish and animated conversation. A coach pulled up at the gate. The panelled hall door swung open. A dapper footman stood regarding us with disdain.

"Excuse me," Mr. Gore addressed the footman. "We have called to visit Granuaile, Queen of Connaught."

"You will locate the O'Malley and her clan, sir, in the library," the footman said impatiently before descending the steps to greet the elegantly dressed party alighting from the gilded coach.

"Good evening, my lord. The Duke and his guests await the pleasure of your company in the ballroom."

We moved into the hall. Thomas, Duke of Ormond, was greeting his guests. Mr. Gore went to speak with Granuaile in the library. Temporarily abandoned, I wandered down the hall.

At the entrance to the lavishly decorated ballroom, sprawled in high-backed armchairs drinking large brandies, were various bohemian poets and playwrights. Inside, positioned strategically in every corner, stood beautiful young debutantes, chaperoned by mothers eager to find suitable husbands for their daughters. These painted and powdered women shamelessly encouraged their reluctant daughters to engage in flirtatious behaviour.

A string quartet began to tune their instruments. A stunning young girl wafted past in a haze of musk. Her flowing gown of maroon taffeta beaded in pearls rustled as she glided across the tiled floor. Her long blonde hair hung in curls over her naked shoulders. Her skin, like her hair, was fair and flawless. It seems unlikely that she had ever exposed her skin to the harmful rays of sunlight. Her slender waist was imprisoned in a tiny corset. Her mother, an elegant lady with a face more pleasing than beautiful and obviously gifted in cunning, spotted a suitor. She guided her daughter towards a distinguished gentleman ladling himself a glass of hot punch from a large and ornate silver bowl. He was bent and wrinkled.

A group of young men gathered around Veronique Jardin, the famous French prima donna. She was tall, thin and beautiful in a moody, intense way.

Mr. Gore appeared at my shoulder.

"I have spoken to Granuaile," he whispered. "She has agreed to grant you a passage to Dublin in return for your interpretative skills tomorrow."

I was confused. Mr. Gore explained.

"Granuaile does not speak English. Queen Elizabeth does not speak Gaelic and you are fluent in both tongues. Granuaile is in the library. She will address you before retiring tonight. I must travel now to my father's home. I will meet you when the Maid of Clew sails."

Granuaile was holding court in the library. Her complexion was weather-beaten and scarred by the harsh salt winds of the Atlantic Ocean. Her dark hair fell long and unkempt around her shoulders. In contrast to the revellers in the ballroom, Granuaile was dressed in a plain, rust-coloured dress with a laced bodice. On her head was a rolled linen head cloth. Seated on the floor at her feet was a young man, a cheeky grin shining through his rust brown beard. He picked up his uileann pipes and placed the thongs around his arm. A distinguished old man sat opposite, crouched over a leather-bound volume of the Bible. He wrote slowly with a goose feather quill. His hands were stained in blue ink.

The musician fingered the chanter and pressed the

bellows. He played masterfully. The hushed attendance radiated contentment. At midnight, during a void in the festivities, Granuaile stood, raised her hand for silence and spoke venomously in Gaelic.

"A chairde, amarach I set sail for my castle home in Clew Bay. Before I do so, I must meet with the Queen of England. It is humiliating, but necessary. I am an old woman and have travelled a great distance to this foreign land to appeal for permission to re-establish my existence in my own country."

Granuaile softened.

"No matter the outcome, friends ... I will carry this precious interlude with me on my final voyage."

Granuaile walked towards the door where I was standing. She was a tall woman and, despite her rugged appearance, attractive. She spoke to me coldly.

"You must be Grainne. Be prepared to travel to Greenwich Castle at first light. We know not the hour when her gracious majesty will summon us," she said sarcastically.

She was a remarkable woman. No precious jewels, fabrics or refinements ... just an extraordinary strength of personality and character.

The library cleared except for the old man, who slept with his Bible clutched to his chest. His forced breathing was disconcerting. I lay upon a gold brocaded couch and drifted to sleep.

CHAPTER 11

I woke as dawn sneaked through a gap in the wooden shutters. My hands and feet were cold. I shivered. the library was freezing. I paced the oak floorboards to the fireplace. The old man who had been sleeping soundly now stirred, exuding a raucous cough. As I tried to revive the embers of the lifeless fire, he eased himself out of the winged chair and shuffled across the room, sniffing, snorting and rolling phlegm around his tongue. Under his arm, he carried his sacred Bible.

As this offensive little man exited the room, Granuaile entered. She was accompanied by a man she introduced as Sir Murrough O'Flaherty. He was a small, plump, dark-haired man with a thick black beard underlining a hooked nose, narrow green penetrating eyes and long, feminine eyelashes. His personality was as off-putting as his appearance. He was instantly dislikeable but, as far as Granuaile was concerned, a necessary evil. His guidance and knowledge of the intricacies of Crown protocol became evident and, ultimately, essential during Granuaile's audience with Queen Elizabeth in Greenwich Castle.

He advised Granuaile intensely as the royal carriage rattled along the cobbled streets of London.

"Queen Elizabeth, the Virgin Queen, is a single-minded

woman of three score years. Her policies on religion and venturesome enterprise have provided England with ideals and aims. She is guided, some say manipulated, by her Privy Council, which is led by the Archbishop of Canterbury. Her policy is to conquer through conciliatory methods. To have you surrender and swear allegiance to the Crown and, in return, simply be re-granted your lands is far less expensive and time-consuming than mobilising and funding an army on foreign soil. The Crown is fearful of Spanish reprisals and the geographical opportunities afforded to her enemies by access through the congenial eastern coast of Ireland. To rule England effectively, she must rule Ireland also. With the support of the Irish chieftains, England reduces the likelihood of a Spanish invasion."

The footman announced our arrival at Greenwich Castle. The palace was a formidable and irregularly shaped building standing on the banks of the River Thames. While the perimeter walls of the castle were fortified with battlements and towers, the interior was more like a riverside manor house. When you passed over the drawbridge, you abandoned the hustle and bustle of crowded London streets and entered a different world. Acres of hothouses, walled gardens and an expansive rolling green pasture spread like a green carpet to the far distant woods.

In the palace courtyard, the coachman pulled up at the entrance to the Royal Apartments. We stood a moment regarding the environment. Greenwich Castle was far removed from the basic stone castles in Ireland. An Irish castle, in contrast, was built essentially as a fortress with comfort at a minimum and security at a maximum.

The Queen's vice chamberlain observed us humorously, then ushered us into a small room, already occupied. There was a milliner and a goldsmith with precious jewels for the Queen's approval. In the corner sat a travelling artist recommended for patronage. The walls and sideboards were decorated with magnificent, richly-coloured tapestries and delicate oriental pottery.

A lady-in-waiting appeared and requested the "Grany Ni Mally party".

"Before you can be presented to Her Majesty, Queen Elizabeth, you must be instructed in royal protocol."

After a few minutes, the vice chamberlain returned and rudely interrupted the lady in waiting. He declared that Her Majesty was now prepared to receive "Grany Ni Mally ".

We followed the vice chamberlain to the Royal Apartments. We walked in single file through a myriad of expansive, tiled corridors abounding with courtiers, emissaries, petitioners and court ladies. We were shown into the anteroom. Here, four maids of honour played cards in a bay window overlooking the river. In a corner, a group of sallow-skinned men spoke in hushed conversation with women bedecked in magnificent jewels. In another corner, a fiddler tuned his instrument while two seamstresses embroidered a satin frilled petticoat.

My instructions were simple: "Speak only if spoken to." Sir Murrough O'Flaherty would stand on Granuaile's right. I would stand two paces behind on her left. The fiddler struck up a tune. Granuaile looked pensive. The vice chamberlain clapped his hands and ushered us through an oak-panelled door. Granuaile regarded him scornfully.

The meeting was held in a long, wood-panelled reception room. Beneath gilded oil portraits stood a dozen court fiddlers in red vests, curious bishops in ornate gold capes and various nobility in dull parliamentary robes. All, including a group of maids of honour, vied for a glimpse of the infamous Pirate Queen. At each end of the room were large, grey marble fireplaces housing roaring log fires. The Queen sat on a crimson velvet armchair beneath a purple and gold canopy.

Granuaile strode confidently through the thousands of flickering candles which lined the walkway to the throne. She was proud and upright as befitted a powerful and notorious leader of men. She wore a long, dark, woollen sleeveless cloak fringed in fine wool that trailed along the ground. The collar was trimmed in a soft and luxurious red fox fur. Underneath, she wore a saffron-coloured linen smock that covered her ankles. The sleeves of the smock were slit, allowing the undershirt to be pulled through. Her bodice was low-cut and laced to below her bosom.

Queen Elizabeth, despite her advancing years, was slim with clear hazel-coloured eyes that were alert and brimming with youthful laughter and excitement She was exquisitely dressed. Her sapphire gown of pure silk had thousands of tiny precious gems laboriously sewn into the seams. Her delicately curled red hair was interwoven with diamonds and moulded with a spray of fine golden hairpins. On her cheek she wore a small black silk patch to compliment her fair complexion.

Granuaile, announced to Queen Elizabeth as "Grany Ni Mally, Queen of Connaught", stepped forward and stood defiantly before the Crown. The Queen, to her credit, ignored this act of defiance and inclined her head with an assurance born from experience, wealth and power. She allowed her feline eyes to roam the room. Both women were vigorous in spirit and health.

Standing before a blazing log fire in a heavy woollen cloak, fashioned to withstand a frigid north wind, Granuaile became noticeably uncomfortable. A lady-in-waiting, seeing that Granuaile was perspiring, offered her a lace handkerchief. Granuaile mopped her brow and tossed the soiled handkerchief into the fire.

"Grany Ni Mally, you are welcome to Greenwich Castle. Your reputation precedes you. But may I query why you should condemn such a fine lace handkerchief to the fire."

Queen Elizabeth spoke to Granuaile in Latin, a language common to both.

"Your Highness, I do not understand the line of your enquiry. That is, unless in our country we have a higher standard of cleanliness. In my household, to pocket a soiled article of such little value is considered unclean."

Granuaile's eyes narrowed. She was mindful that others before her had been beheaded for such irreverence to the Queen of England. Granuaile grasped the initiative and added, "Your Highness, I sought this audience to discuss far more important matters. I humbly request that you allow me to continue to serve the Crown by expelling those of your enemies who seek to gain a foothold in England through the western coastline of Ireland. I will, if permitted in your name, put these hostile factions to the sword."

Queen Elizabeth listened with interest, admiration and compassion. Her greatest fear was that the Spanish would attempt to access a vulnerable and unguarded English coastline through Ireland. Harnessing and utilising Granuaile's influence over the western coastline of Ireland was a far more positive and cost-effective solution than imprisonment.

"In return," Granuaile continued, "I request maintenance and my legal entitlement to the thirds of both of my husband's estates."

Queen Elizabeth sat impassively as Granuaile bowed and retreated, awaiting her judgement.

"Grany Ni Mally, you stand before me as the self-appointed Queen of Connaught. Over the centuries, your clan have patrolled the western seas of Ireland, pirating and plundering all who dared sail those perilous waters. Your wealth was gained at the misfortune of others. Nevertheless, like you, I am a practical woman. I believe that a nation should be guided rather than coerced. Can you satisfy me of your intention to remain a loyal servant?"

Granuaile raised her head and, holding a silver crucifix, earnestly replied, "I swear by the Holy Trinity, and by this crucifix, that I will bear faith and true allegiance to my sovereign. I pledge to serve the Crown unto death, so help me God."

The Queen stood.

"Grany Ni Mally, by the power vested in me and in return for your humble pledge of loyalty and subject to your agreement to rule your lands by English laws and customs, I grant you the portions of your estates that are your entitlement. The amount received in maintenance from these estates is to be deducted from the taxes payable to the state. I will send a communication this day to Sir Richard Bingham informing him of the Crown's rulings. I will instruct him that your son and brother are to be released on receipt of same communication."

Granuaile bowed. The audience over, we followed protocol and backed into the anteroom. Queen Elizabeth had effectively granted Granuaile permission to return to her old trade under the guise of protecting the Crown.

Two hours later, in jubilant mood, we boarded Granuaile's three mast galley, the Maid of Clew, which was berthed below London Bridge. First Lieutenant Mr. Gore stood on the poop deck directing operations. I was delighted and relieved to see him.

The wooden galley, the Maid of Clew, was an ocean-going ship of similar design to those of the Spanish armada. It was built for its ability to sail in and out of the rocks and shallow waters of Clew Bay, where larger vessels inevitably floundered. Fore and aft, there were bronze and iron swivel guns. It was ninety feet long and twenty-five feet wide. Below deck, on both the port and starboard sides, were rows of twelve gun ports. On the upper gun deck there were five smaller cannons. Including the stern, there were forty cannons in all on board. The main mast was ninety feet high. The fore and mizzen masts were shorter at sixty feet. It was the flagship of Granuaile's fleet of nine galleys and six merchant ships. It carried up to two hundred fighting men and only required a working crew of fifty men. It was, of course, no match for the enormous English warships carrying up to one thousand men.

As we were piped aboard Granuaile instructed Mr. Gore.

"Mr. Gore make a signal to the flag to make ready!"

CHAPTER 12

The flags soaring above the Maid of Clew signalled the intentions of her captain to make ready to sail. Members of the crew who had been idling on the quay side came running up the gangway. The cook, an overweight foul-smelling man with a hideously deformed red nose and a peg leg, came aboard first. He was clutching two long, thin cages stuffed with terrified chickens flapping their crudely clipped wings. He placed them in a long boat on the open deck beside two tethered goats and four pigs in a wooden corral. Mr. Gore told me that he was chosen as cook not for his culinary skills but due to the fact that, with his wooden leg, he could do nothing else. His function was to manage and distribute the ship's provisions of salted fish, beef, pork and, of course, the most important commodity of all on the ocean ... drinking water.

The ship's carpenter, his hands covered with calluses, reached for the weather rail. The physician, who acted as both doctor and dentist, followed. Bringing up the rear was a young gunner, three of his fingers missing and his youthful face scorched and scarred by gunpowder.

"Anchor's hove short ... All stores secured ... God speed and good luck ... Hands aloft, loose top sails."

The anchors were raised and the goatskin portolanos, a

map detailing the coastline features in sequence, was laid out. The Maid of Clew headed downstream, threading through heavy traffic. We were heading for the Nore, a sandy islet. Here we were to wait for the two warships assigned to convey us safely through the Irish sea.

When we arrived at the Nore, there were up to one hundred vessels anchored and waiting to form convoys. While we waited, the ship rocked in a garland of slime and weed. Two sloops of war arrived and indicated that they were bound for northern Scotland and Ireland. They requested the transpire, a customs document detailing our cargo.

"Break out the anchor," a barrel-chested boatswain roared. "Heave men, heave!"

"Anchors away."

Seven vessels, including ourselves, moved off eastward. We were clustered around the two sloops like goslings around parent geese. The rigging and the shrouds came alive with swarming figures as men ran aloft as surefooted as cats.

"Mr. Gore," Granuaile remarked looking at the assortment of slow-moving cargo ships, "our progress will be severely hampered because there are few sailing ships in our convoy."

The Maid of Clew heeled sharply as a gust of wind held her.

"Man the braces. Look alive."

I stood on the poop deck as we sailed up the Thames. Playful children ran along the wooded river bank. Wind filled the rebellious sails and the billowing canvas thundered out hard and full. The ship creaked and banged. The shrouds and rigging whined like the strings of a mad orchestra. The bow began throwing back spray. It was cold, but exhilarating. The boat turned and bit into the first angry swell. Mr. Gore climbed into the shrouds.

Life at sea was interesting at first, then boring and, finally, hazardous. Sea sickness was a major problem, even for seasoned sailors. Hygiene was always at a minimum. Sewage, in calm weather, was dispensed over the side. In bad weather, it was thrown into the hold along with the stores of food and water. There were no lavatories, just heads, which were holes cut in the deck planking with a crude seat built above. Disease on board killed slowly. Some sailors carried rare tropical diseases, others suffered from scurvy due to vitamin C deficiency. These unfortunate sailors were deathly pale, gaunt and in constant muscular pain. Eventually, at best they lost their teeth, at worst their lives. I was convinced that the practice of allowing the sailors to carry exotic pets, like monkeys and birds bought or stolen in foreign ports, contributed to many of their deaths. Mr. Gore told me that for every man that died in battle forty died of disease.

Clothes that were washed in seawater shrank and never dried properly unless they were soaked in urine first. Fresh water, the most important commodity on board, was rationed. After a couple days at sea, however, it turned green and slimy. The warm, rancid beer tasted better. At sea, food was a necessity and never enjoyable. There were limited cooking facilities and the only palatable meal was a thick pea soup. There was no bread, only biscuits. The men below deck joked that they shared their meals with rats, maggots and weevils while the captain enjoyed fresh meat and eggs. Often the biscuits made from flour and water were alive with squirming maggots. The only way to limit the number of maggots was to place a large dead fish into the sack of biscuits. The maggots would then crawl out to eat the fish. When the fish was covered, it was removed and replaced with a fresh one. The salted meat had to be steeped in water to remove the preservatives. It was tough and very dry, but not as tough as the cheese, which some of the sailors carved into ornaments. The daily rationed diet consisted of dried peas, salt pork or beef, cheese, a bowl of oatmeal and eight pints of ale. The men used their hands to eat and their greasy neckscarves to wipe their fingers.

Below deck, the air was damp and the conditions atrocious. There was little ventilation as hundreds of hot, sweaty, foul-smelling bodies moved and toiled in cramped conditions. The men seldom wore shirts. They were proud to display the varied tattoos that emblazoned their sinewy, muscular bodies. During the day, the off-duty men would sit while the tattooist, armed with coloured inks and ash, pricked out patterns in the sailors' skin.

The most hideous smells emanated from the ballast in the hold. The ballast, which kept the ship upright, consisted of loose stones called shingle. Everything drained into the hold and, as a consequence, it constituted a grave health risk. Each week, it was fumigated by sprinkling vinegar and sulphur over hot coals. The clouds of poisonous gas apparently cleansed the hold. It did not, unfortunately, kill the hundreds of rats that lived in the rotten debris.

"It becomes increasingly hard to understand why any man should, of his own free will, take to the sea," Mr. Gore exclaimed. "They appear from nowhere and are inevitably bound for nowhere."

Above deck, the men toiled on four hour shifts. One sailor, the timekeeper, used a sand-filled timer to measure each half hour and broadcast the time by ringing the ship's bell. The sailors had many daily jobs, from scrubbing the decks with a block of sandstone to washing the hammocks. The Maid of Clew required constant attention. The helmsman at the wheel had to ensure that he steered the ship on the correct course and the captain had to provide the correct combination of sails to best harness the wind. Too little sail and the ship did not move fast enough through the water. Too much and a strong gust of wind could snap a mast. To adjust a sail, the crew had to climb to the yard, the horizontal bar that supported the sail, and either increase or decrease the area of sail exposed to the wind. The sailors who worked high above in the rigging did so without safety nets. Often in the rush to go aloft to loose sails, mistakes were made and, in this case, the unfortunate man either plunged into the icy sea or crashed with a sickening thud onto the deck below.

After three days at sea, as darkness fell, Granuaile issued an order.

"Break from the convoy, Mr. Gore."

"It is a brave order," Mr. Gore confided. "These are treacherous waters for a ship moderately armed. The Irish Sea is riddled with privateers, pirates licensed by their governments to raid factions they consider hostile."

The following morning I stood at the helm, staring across the tumbling waste of seawater. The drummer heralded daybreak. Granuaile raised her glasses. In the strengthening light, a ship came into focus. I could just make out her tall pyramid of full sails and the spray dancing around her bow. The ship flew the Queen's flag, but Granuaile looked concerned.

"All hands! ... all hands on deck!" she roared.

Below deck, her call was repeated. Men stumbled from their hammocks. Mr. Gore appeared, bleary-eyed. Granuaile pointed at the oncoming galley. He looked through his glasses.

"She is going about, captain," Mr. Gore said, sensing Granuaile's concern.

The main deck was alive with seamen pointing at the fast-approaching galley. They chattered nervously. I blinked away sea spray. Mr. Gore closed the eye glass with a snap. The approaching ship had completed its manoeuvre and now settled on a direct course for the Maid of Clew.

"Mr. Gore, although this ship flies the Queen's flag, my intuition tells me something is amiss. Have the gunners make ready."

"Clear for action. Have the guns loaded!" Mr. Gore roared.

Granuaile's manner was, as always, disconcerting, but her controlled demeanour was comforting.

"Main top'l braces. Look alive men!"

The sails were flapping and thundering as the Maid of Clew swung into the wind. I felt ill and went below. When I returned, Granuaile stood with Mr. Gore, her fox fur collar pulled around her ears. Both of them were transfixed as they observed the approaching ship. From above, the shrill voice of the signal man called out.

"Captain, the Prince Regent is signalling that she has urgent dispatches. She requests permission to board."

The Prince Regent altered its course. Its bow was almost at right angles to the Maid of Clew. Granuaile reflected, then followed her instincts.

"Guns loaded and prepared to be run out, captain!" came the call from below.

"Mr. Gore, stand by to go about."

Mr. Gore's training and respect for Granuaile was such that he did not question her orders. The Maid of Clew laboured around. The years of sail drill in all weathers paid instant dividends as the confused sailors tugged at sheets and braces.

Granuaile's instincts were sound. The Prince Regent now ran up a new set of colours. Her ports opened, concealed cannons trundled outwards. The Maid of Clew steadied on her new course, then surged as the gun crews

106

rushed to their positions.

The Prince Regent, her sails flapping furiously, headed into the wind and turned on the same circle. Mr. Gore spoke to Granuaile.

"We owe our lives to your intuition, captain! If we had not altered course on your command, the Prince Regent would surely have crossed our bows and poured sufficient shot to destroy the Maid of Clew."

"Mr. Gore," Granuaile replied cynically, "your words of praise are premature. Ahead you see a deep keeled warship. Regard the crouching gunners, the colourful clusters of officers and the rows of cannons. The Maid of Clew is little more than a merchant ship!" Granuaile shifted position and, grasping a handrail, added, "The Prince Regent will attempt to regain her first advantage. The wind is in her favour. A confrontation is inevitable. We must prepare the men for battle."

"Run out guns and prepare to fire," Mr. Gore ordered.

"Cleared for action, sir," came the cry from below. Men ran the length of the decks throwing down sand to allow the gunners a firm grip.

"We must, Mr. Gore, put our fate in your judgement," Granuaile said. "Below there are many new men, some of whom stare without comprehension, others in animal fear. We must hope that when the battle commences they will carry out their orders with distinction. The Prince Regent, you may be assured,will have an experienced crew of seasoned sailors and deserters who will be no strangers to battle."

Granuaile looked long and hard at Mr. Gore. He was aware that she was searching for possible weaknesses. He walked to the weather rail and shouted along the deck.

"Gather round, men."

The men ran obediently to where Mr. Gore stood on the

poop deck.

"We are destined to do battle with the warship Prince Regent. No matter what, you must obey and trust your orders. Granuaile, chief of the O'Malley clan, is the most famous sea captain in these waters and will, I am confident, extricate us from this battle with credit ... Be mindful also that this is an O'Malley galley and there will be no surrender."

The crew cheered. Mr. Gore thrust his hands beneath the tails of his coat and returned to the stern.

"In a moment," Granuaile ordered, "we will beat to windward, Mr. Gore. And," she added, "we must draw first blood."

With a groan and an explosion of canvas, the Maid of Clew altered her course again. I went below. Crouching behind a cannon, my hands resting upon my knees, I stared fixedly through the open port. In spite of the sea breeze that blew through the opening, I began to perspire. My heart pumped against my ribcage like the beating of a drum. I was a helpless victim of a stark nightmare. All around, men squatted, devoid of expression, waiting for the command to fire. At each cannon there was a six man crew. The gun captain primed, aimed and fired the gun. The other men turned and raised the gun barrel, loaded the ammunition and damped down sparks. Because gunpowder is so inflammable, the gun crews kept very few cartridges close to the cannons so the powder monkey, a young boy, had to run continually to the handling chamber for fresh gunpowder.

Above, I could see Mr. Gore, his palms resting on the smooth wood of the handrail, his eyes fixed in the direction of the Prince Regent. Granuaile came below and spoke to her crew.

"Men," she roared, "listen carefully to what I have to

say. We will soon be firing a broadside on the Prince Regent." She looked at each man in turn, still searching for weakness. "We may not boast as many cannons as the Prince Regent, but if we load twice as quickly, we will drastically reduce their numerical advantage. Move with purpose and remember, it is imperative that you follow orders and ignore the clamour and confusion that will erupt and envelop you. There will be no surrender. I will personally cut the throat of any sailor who places the life of another in jeopardy through cowardice!"

Faces gleaming in sweat and fear acknowledged their esteemed captain before turning back to stare out through the gun port at the empty sea.

"We are outclassed and outgunned," a man behind me whispered. "It is only a matter of time."

One of the experienced gunners advised me to wrap a scarf around my ears. Above, there was a rasp of steel as Mr. Gore drew his sword.

"Put the helm down! Hard down!" roared Granuaile.

The Maid of Clew swung wildly across the wind. Instantly, the raked bow of the Prince Regent came into view, her hull soaked with spray. Mr. Gore dropped his sword.

"Fire!"

The Maid of Clew recoiled as the row of cannons exploded. The ship lurched backwards in a staggering, thunderous roar. Choking smoke billowed back through the ports, raking at my lungs and eyes. As the smoke cleared, the men cleaned the gun and damped down the sparks to prevent an explosion during reloading. The cannon was loaded with shot and gunpowder and a quill filled with powder was inserted as a fuse. Using handspikes and ropes, they levered the guns back into position. The bow of the Prince Regent was framed in the port.

"Fire!"

The gun captain lit the fuse and the men jumped out of the way and covered their ears. The violent explosion blasted the cannon backwards. Again, the Maid of Clew heaved beneath us. My whole being shook with the hellish roar of the guns. My eyes and lungs were rasped. This time, I could clearly hear the Maid of Clew's cannon balls strike home.

The Prince Regent returned fire. A hot wind crossed above the Maid of Clew. From aloft came a falling tangle of severed halyards and ropes.

"They fired too soon," came the joyous cry from above.

"Mr. Gore," roared Granuaile, pointing at the masthead pendant, "the wind is veering … The Prince Regent is in irons."

The Prince Regent had met the full wind hard across her bow. At first it looked as if she might rally, but the wind eluded her. The Prince Regent was now steadfast.

"Stand by to go about, Mr. Gore."

Men clambered aloft to splice the severed lines.

"She is under way again," came the cry from above. "Prepare to fire before she completes her turn!"

We met the Prince Regent broadside but, before Mr. Gore could issue the order, the enemy ship belched fire and smoke along the long line of her ports. This time, there was no mistake and the hull shuddered and reeled backwards from the force. Cannon balls screamed through the air, crashing into and splintering the woodwork and rigging. There was pandemonium. I could see nothing in the thick black smoke. Men were crying out for help. Flying splinters ripped into the flesh of the gunners crouched before their cannons. The deck turned red with blood. When the smoke cleared, I found myself covered in specks of blood and gristle. A gunner sat opposite, both his legs blown clear away.

A young boy clung to him, screaming uncontrollably.

Close to the waterline, the carpenter and his mate ran along the hull nailing timber and lead over the holes. I clambered above. As I did, another ragged volley crashed into the Maid of Clew. Below, men cursed and fumbled blindly in the smoke. Above, in terror, a sailor ran across the deck. As he did, an eighteen pound cannon ball screamed through the air and appeared to cut him in half. I turned away, fighting nausea. Curious, I turned back. The man's head and shoulders remained upright on the planking. His eyes were open and staring at his severed trunk which was tangled in the rigging.

"Fire ... Mr. Gore ... Fire!"

A volley of shot returned through the smoke in the direction of the Prince Regent. A man fell from the rigging above my head and landed in a sickening thud at my feet. A sailor screamed and leaned over a weather rail, a long wooden splinter deeply imbedded in his shoulder. Through the blood, I could see the thick stump of jagged timber buried deep in his neck. Below, I saw the gunner with the missing fingers spit on his cannon. The spittle hissed on the hot barrel. A cannon ball crashed through the port and struck the young sailor on the side of the head, killing him instantly.

There was a splintering crack from above. Looking up through the drifting smoke, I could see that another volley from the Prince Regent had struck the foremast. The shattered mast broke away and the intricate spray of rigging and canvas fell into the sea. Tangled like a fly in a spider's web, his head suspended above the foaming surf, was a sailor. The torn sail ballooned in the water and began to drag at the ship like an anchor.

"Mr. Gore," Granuaile yelled, "fetch axes and cut the wreckage adrift."

"Shipmates," the terrified sailor cried from below as the men attacked the rigging with axes, "help me. Don't let me ..."

The condemned man stared up with mad eyes at his comrades. In a pitiful final gesture, he shook his fist. Moments later, the sail, engulfed with water, began to sink. The man's legs continued to wriggle as he disappeared, head first, below the surf.

All around, men crouched and whimpered. The screaming of the wounded as they were taken below to the physician was blood-curdling. All through, Granuaile stood erect, her cloak stained with gunpowder and blood. Her detached, but determined, expression never changed.

The advantages gained at the outset were now completely lost. The Prince Regent maintained a steady barrage of fire across the decks of the Maid of Clew. The enemy were now firing high into the rigging, attempting to render the Maid of Clew immobile by slashing what remained of her sails. This was a common tactic used when the captain wished to disarm and capture a ship rather than destroy it.

The windless sails began to flap. Granuaile, unyielding and unmoved, observed the pulped remains of her dead sailors on the deck. Many of her men died bravely, their mutilated and shattered bodies writhing in agony. Others, not so brave, cowered among the dead. She shifted her gaze above the bank of smoke to the punctured sails.

"Mr. Gore, send more men aloft to splice the mizzen shrouds!"

Granuaile stood alone, grim but unflinching. She was clearly agitated. This was to have been her final triumphant voyage. Breaking from the convoy was a serious error of judgement and she was now paying the ultimate price.

"The only alternative to death," she roared across the

stern to Mr. Gore, "is failure and disgrace."

"Watch your helm ... Steady as you go!" Mr. Gore warned the helmsman. His command fell on deaf ears. The man lay dead upon the deck, blood trickling from his mouth. There was a gaping hole in the centre of his forehead. Another sailor, chewing earnestly on a wad of tobacco, took his place.

"We must," Granuaile instructed, "aim a final broadside across the stern of the Prince Regent." Her tone was cold and final.

"Mr. Gore, Mr. Gore! The wheel ... Mr. Gore, it does not respond!" the helmsman was roaring despairingly. The wheel spun in his hands without altering the ship's course. The Maid of Clew was at the mercy of the sea and the Prince Regent.

Granuaile cupped her hands: "Cease firing!"

The silence was as frightening as the gunfire that had preceded it. I could hear the water lap against the side of the ship, the clatter of loose rigging and the moaning of the injured. Mr. Gore turned to Granuaile for guidance. Across the water, drifting towards us in the grey smoke, was the sound of men cheering. Moments later, the raked bow of the Prince Regent broke through the smoke. Men could be seen running forward to where the ships would meet. Others prepared to lash the warring ships together in a final embrace.

"Mr. Gore." The sharpness in Granuaile's voice made him jump. "Load every starboard gun with chain shot."

"Men," Mr. Gore called out, "gather your strength for one final foray. Each gun must be loaded with chain shot and each weapon then set at full elevation. Load, but do not run out until I give the order!"

The men carried the unwieldy chain shot - two cannon balls linked together with a thick chain. There was barely thirty feet of water now between the two ships. The Prince Regent came ever closer, her rigging alive with boisterous, excited men.

"Mr. Gore, the captain of the Prince Regent must have stripped his guns of men to raise such a large boarding party," Granuaile noted.

Pistol shots rang out. The boarding party from the Prince Regent yelled in derision and flexed their muscles. The gunners below waited anxiously for the command to fire.

"Run out the guns! ... Run out the guns! ... Stand firm, men! Fire! ... All guns fire!"

The Maid of Clew recoiled as the whole battery of guns exploded beneath our feet. The force of the explosion drove the warring ships apart. I fell backwards against the weather rail. The air came alive as the chain shot scythed through man, sail and rigging. The deck of the Prince Regent was, in an instant, a tangled bloody mess of cries and curses as the boarders were cut down. The whirling chain shot, in a tempest of metal, cut through mast and sail, the falling canvas obscuring her gun ports.

"Reload. Continue to fire!"

A trail of floating wreckage and corpses now spanned the two ships. Resounding cheers gave way to screams of pain and confusion.

"Fire!"

One final ragged salvo. My heart thumped and my eyes filled with tears of emotion and strain. Before us, the Prince Regent turned. From above and below deck, men came to the weather rails. Some sobbed uncontrollably, others danced on the smoking, bloodstained decks. Everyone was gratified that the enemy had been repelled and turned to Granuaile.

"Thank you gentlemen," she looked along the decks,

"you are a credit to your profession."

Mr. Gore removed his hat and shook Granuaile's hand.

An hour later, relief gave way to delayed shock. The dead were gathered. Lines of men scrubbed the blood-stained decks, brushing the bright red sand overboard. The sail makers sat cross-legged, their needles patching ravaged canvas The carpenter surveyed the masts and splintered planking. I leaned heavily on a rail, my legs weak from fatigue and strain. It had been a long day and sleep beckoned. I went below.

CHAPTER 13

The following morning, a still, cold dawn promised a wilder day to follow. We were locked in an aggravated swell. A sky of dirty grey swirled and blotted out the rising sun. The dense cloud reached to the very surface of the sea. Somewhere in the dark emptiness beyond the horizon, the sun was rising. Here there was no horizon, no dawn and no sky. As the day wore on, the contrary winds and tides seemed to have us blundering backwards more than forwards. Uninterrupted by any land mass, the atmospheric depression swept across the cold, open sea. The wave patterns slowly built up into a succession of marching mountain ranges.

The men were tired and hungry. They had worked through the night repairing the ship. They were chilled to the bone and their fingers were stiff and bleeding. Tempers were beginning to flare. Earlier, in an emotional ceremony, the crew had watched the remains of their comrades and friends, wrapped in sailcloth, slip from the decks of the Maid of Clew into the Irish Sea. The mournful strains of the uileann pipes still haunted the ship. Below, the possessions of the dead sailors were auctioned. The proceeds were to be dispatched to the men's families when the ship next docked.

The clouds overhead had turned an angry purple colour. The experienced sailors read the signs and looked worried.

"Baton down the hatches. Secure rations!" Granuaile ordered.

Below, the bloodied scars of battle still lined the timbers. The sails above thundered and the deck groaned as the bow of the galley burst through each wave crest in an explosion of white foam. My gut began to heave and my legs buckle. The Maid of Clew was floundering. The sea coming aboard was grey and hostile. The helmsman was roped to the wheel. The captain remained vigilant.

"Lord be merciful," I heard her cry.

The Maid of Clew twisted and dropped into deep valleys of foaming sea. We climbed slowly and, on reaching the crest, hurtled downwards into the depths at breakneck speed. At the bottom, the water rose before us in a mountainous grey wall.

Suddenly, there was a grating sound as if a sand bank had moulded itself to the hull of the ship. We had run aground … I looked over the weather rail through eyes inflamed from salted spray.

"Oh no, not again!" I cried.

Fortunately, an enormous wave rose up underneath the bow, crashed down on the deck of the besieged Maid of Clew and propelled the stricken galley back out to sea. The storm was now unleashing its full strength. Men, with terror in their eyes, climbed high into the riggings to trim sails. The ship groaned under the endless assault of wind and sea. Thunder cannoned above. Brilliant cascades of lightning lit up the grey sky. My head hit something with a numbing shock. My vision began to swirl in flashing colour and light. Through a haze of wind, rain and spray, a cannon fired. Then, from the mizzen, came the anguished, but relieved, cry:

"Land ahoy, captain! Land ahoy!"

The Maid of Clew limped, impotent but triumphant, into Howth harbour. Above, shrouded in mist, stood Howth Castle. Granuaile ordered Mr. Gore to make ready to sail for the Isle of Aran at first light, then marched to the castle with a small party of men.

Granuaile approached the imposing gates of the castle. They passed an elderly footman leading a curious young boy on a grey pony. The gates of the castle opened. The steward presented himself.

"Good day, sir," Granuaile declared, "I am Grace O'Malley, Queen of Connaught. My galley, which has been incessantly stormed by untamed man and sea, lies despondent in the harbour. We have berthed in Howth to seek respite and to replenish our provisions. I have taken this opportunity to call socially on the Lord of Howth."

"Wait here, Ma'am. I will inform his lordship of your visit."

Within minutes the steward returned.

"His lordship is dining and does not wish to be disturbed."

Without uttering another word, the steward locked the gate. Granuaile was furious and returned immediately to the Maid of Clew. On the quay, Granuaile spoke to the curious young boy,who was inspecting the damaged Maid of Clew.

"Good day, young man. That is a fine pony you are riding. Is she yours?" Granuaile queried.

"Yes, Ma'am, and thank you. My father gave her to me as a gift," the boy replied, running his fingers nervously through the pony's long, dark mane.

"Your father must be a wealthy man to afford such fine pony?" Granuaile enquired sharply.

"The Lord of Howth, Ma'am, is the wealthiest man in

Ireland!" the boy replied boastfully.

"I wonder then," said Granuaile, "what value he will put on his son's life?"

In an instant, on Granuaile's instructions, the startled footman and the boy were bound and placed in the hold of the Maid of Clew.

"Mr. Gore, make ready to sail."

Mr. Gore regarded the exchange on the quay as I did - with disdain. He approached Granuaile.

"I cannot be a party to such a deed. It is a hideous act of little credit. It can only succeed in drawing the wrath of judgement upon us. While I respect your ability, madame, as a sea captain, I must humbly request that, if it is your intention to sail from Howth with the boy as your hostage, I may be relieved of my duties."

"I cannot abide a man who has not the stomach for fair and open conflict," Granuaile roared. "You and what is left of your men and this useless girl are, as requested, relieved of your duties this instant. Bear witness, Mr. Gore. Never again will the gates of Howth Castle be closed to an O'Malley."

Granuaile turned and issued orders to raise the flag and prepare to cast off.

We watched from the cold, windswept headland as the Maid of Clew crawled from the harbour, her patched sails billowing as she set a course for the Isle of Aran. Mr. Gore and the men he had extricated from various lodgings and taverns in London set out for Dublin.

We marched for over an hour along the headland, crossing sandy beaches and marsh until, in the distance, we sighted a church spire. It began to rain. Torrents of hail pounded us. We moved to the church for shelter. As we neared the old building, a volley of shots was unleashed. Mr. Gore ordered his men to take cover. He crawled

119

onwards through the gorse and wet grass. Below him, in a hollow bordered by pine trees, was a small, stone-built country church. In the cemetery, crouched behind grave stones, was a company of English soldiers. They fired a continuous barrage of lead at the church walls. Surrounded and taking refuge was a company of foreign sailors. In the bay, a small galley flying a Spanish flag pulled against its anchors. On the strand were three long boats. Mr. Gore returned and addressed the men.

"Gentlemen, the Crown, I believe, has inadvertently offered us the opportunity to strike out in our own right. A Spanish galley lies anchored in the bay. Her officers and men are below in the church grounds, under siege. While they are grounded, their ship is vulnerable. I estimate that they have left only a token number of men aboard. I propose that, under the cover of darkness, we utilise the element of surprise and take the ship."

That afternoon, we sat and waited for nightfall, huddled together in the scrub playing cards and dice. Before us, in the bay, the Spanish galley strained at its anchors. Behind, we heard spasmodic, but continuous, pistol fire. As darkness enveloped us, Mr. Gore gave the order to make for the boats. For a moment there was a strange air of tension until one of the older and more respected sailors stood and saluted.

"Aye, aye, captain!"

We hurried across the beach and launched the Spanish long boats. Not a sound was uttered as we rowed out to the ship. We circled the galley. The water lapped gently against the hull. An agile young sailor clambered up the stern and secured a rope ladder for those who were less nimble. I remained in the long boat as the rest of the men boarded.

In a moment, the silence was broken as a man surged forward from the quarter deck to repel the boarders. Mr.

Gore raised his sword and cut the man down. Another pitched forward from the direction of the hold. He was taken from behind with an axe. Suddenly, pistol and musket shot sparked and whistled around the deck. A man staggered forward, his breeches and coat covered in blood and flesh. He opened his mouth and blood and spit trickled forth. He fell awkwardly to the deck. A salvo of musket fire crossed the bow. A man fell squirming, his flesh pulped and singed. A cannon fired. The ball crashed into the mast, splintering a large section. A sailor ran screaming, his eyes blinded by flying splinters. As quickly as the skirmish had begun, it ceased.

There was a commotion from the bow of the ship. Curious, I climbed the rope ladder. A giant sailor appeared before me, close to the stern. He was dragging Mr. Gore. The huge sailor held a jagged knife to Mr. Gore's throat. He grinned. Mr. Gore's sword fell to the deck. The sailor kicked it away. He appeared eager to kill. There was the distinct air of madness about him. I returned and stood motionless in the long boat ... watching. The sailor led Mr. Gore to the stern. Without releasing his hold, he climbed over the weather rail, a muscular arm encircling Mr. Gore's neck. With little effort, he raised his hostage clear off the deck and over the weather rail. They descended backwards down the swaying rope ladder into the longboat.

I reached back and grasped the carpenter's claw hammer. As the sailor turned to step into the long boat I brought the blunt head of the instrument down as hard as I could on the back of his skull. The sailor's head cracked and jerked forward, smashing against the hull. I struck him again, this time with the claw end of the hammer. The enraged man turned, lost his footing and fell backwards into the sea, the hammer imbedded in his skull. After a few moments, a sailor above aimed and fired a musket at the

121

lifeless body in the sea.

"He will make a tasty morsel for the fish!" Mr. Gore exclaimed as the tide carried the dead sailor out to sea. The other dead and injured Spanish sailors were bound and placed in one of the long boats.

Mr. Gore gauged the wind against his cheek and looked above to the masthead pendant. The wind was rising. Everyone was eager to set sail.

"Break out the anchor … Lay a course south, past the headland and on to the east coast port of Wicklow," roared Mr. Gore.

I was on my way home. It would not be long now.

"Loose head sails!"

The cry was passed along the deck like a chant. High above, the sails flapped and banged as the wind took hold. Men, strung out precariously on the yards, grappled with flying canvas. Being short-handed, they had to run from one job to the next. The men below, their muscles and lungs straining, pulled at ropes. From out of the night sky came men sliding down the stays to add their weight. Mr. Gore stood proudly, watching his men respond willingly and effectively to his orders. He proudly looked above to the spiralling masthead of his first command, sucked in the cold night air and bit his lip.

"Let her run freely, double the lookouts and beware. Every ship in the Irish sea is a mortal enemy."

"I will have you home by daybreak," Mr. Gore said smiling.

"Thank you, captain" I replied.

CHAPTER 14

Mr. Gore pulled his cloak up around his shoulders. The freshening wind pushed away the grey clouds that hung on the bow of the galley. I looked at him. He had aged. The men lowered a long boat. Wicklow lay somewhere beyond the mist. I stood on the splintered deck. For a brief moment, I considered remaining with the galley and sailing on to Portugal. My nostrils were still filled with smoke and gunpowder. My throat was dry, my mind blank.

Mr. Gore swallowed hard, turned away and looked out to sea. It was time for me to disembark. He seemed distant, almost cold. He escorted me to the stern. It was an awkward moment. He was detached, just like … Granuaile. We simply shook hands.

I was put down on the shore close to the Murrough. The sea mist was rising. In the distance, I could distinguish the outline of Mountclare Castle. The water lapped gently on the shingle. Mr. Gore stood proud and erect on the bridge. I sat on the damp sand and watched as the galley turned majestically and headed out to sea. I heard for the last time the groaning timbers and the thunder as the wind grasped the sails.

"Anchor's hove short, sir! All stores secured!"
"Lay a course for the Bay of Biscay!"

"Aye aye, captain!"

Mr. Gore turned towards the shore. He tipped his hat. I sat there until the galley merged with the horizon, my emotions as scattered as the damp grains of sand that ran through my fingers.

The wind began to rise. The silence was broken by the sound of dogs barking. Two men appeared on horseback. I ran into the dunes and hid among the ferns. I allowed them to pass before setting off across the fields for the castle.

Nearer the castle, I realised that something was wrong. The air was filled with the rancid odour of damp, burning timber. I picked my way slowly through the gloomy forest until I reached a clearing. There before me was Mountclare Castle. Its contents were laid bare, smouldering on the ramparts. Its walls were indelibly scorched. The castle was deserted. I ran to the moat. All that remained of the drawbridge was a single badly-charred plank. I edged across into the compound. The castle was a smouldering shell.

My past - or was it my future? - now lay in ashes. I felt an anger forged in despair and helplessness surging up inside me. I picked up a large stone and hurled it with all my might against the castle wall. I then reached for the Key to the Past. It still hung securely on a chain around my neck. But was my tenuous link with the future broken?

From high above, there was a movement. The stump of a timber beam broke from the wall. A barrage of stones and debris hailed down upon me. My head exploded in a symphony of bright lights and searing pain.